Other titles available in the Savannah Stories:

Blast From The Past

Payback

First Comes Love

Tainted Love

Walking On Broken Glass

Other titles by J.L. Lemon:

Second Chances

The Savannah Stories

Angel Unaware

The Savannah Stories

Angel Unaware

J.L. LEMON

ISBN-13: 978-0-9796117-6-6
ISBN-10:   0-9796117-6-8

Published 2008

Printed by Lulu.com in the United States of America

To my parents. I am truly blessed and I love you.

And…

To all who have encouraged my writing and who continue to read it.

I thank you all.

Dear Reader,

Thank you for choosing to read "Angel Unaware". This story places Savannah in a situation all too many women find themselves. While there are many different reactions to being diagnosed with cancer or any other serious illness, Savannah's reaction is uniquely hers but still she faces the same feelings all women do.

I wanted the story set at Christmas because it is associated with hope, love and faith. When we face adversity, I believe God sends angels to reassure us and let us know that not only He is with us, but we have guardian angels to guide us as well. I like to believe that these angels are our loved ones that have gone before us.

Another reason I set the story at Christmas is that it's a time when we remember the ones who have passed on. When we converse about them and recall those special moments, they continue to live through our memories. This story is a bit fantasy, a lot reality but mostly about hope and faith. Savannah faces an uncertain future and she wishes she could turn to the loving arms of her mother for comfort. I wanted to write a story that showed, despite the fact our loved ones, though gone from our sight, still live in our hearts and love us from beyond.

I hope you enjoy reading it.

J.L. Lemon

What Cancer Cannot Do

Cancer is so limited

Cancer cannot cripple love

Cancer cannot shatter hope

Cancer cannot erode faith

Cancer cannot destroy peace

Cancer cannot kill friendship

Cancer cannot destroy memories

Cancer cannot silence courage

Cancer cannot invade the soul

Cancer cannot steal eternal life

Cancer cannot conquer the spirit

Cancer is so limited…

Author Unknown

"Be not forgetful to entertain strangers:

for thereby some have entertained angels unaware."

Hebrews 13:2

1

Christmas Eve

Lenox Square Mall was the last place Savannah wanted to be. Sure it was located in a ritzy part of Atlanta near the famed Buckhead addition and it touted big name stores that carried tons of specialty items. Mostly items she couldn't afford but that was another story. Obviously plenty of people could afford Lenox Square because the place was literally crawling with shoppers judging by the parking lot. Impatient fathers, weary mothers and loud, excited children could be seen marching their way toward the huge mall like ants to a piece of candy.

Between that and the general Christmas hustle and bustle, all facets added up to misery and Savannah felt more than sufficiently miserable. As she and Ennis traveled literally acres of parking lot to find an open parking space, Ennis finally gave up and pulled to the curb at the main entrance.

Savannah pointed to a sign directly in front of them, "You do realize you parked in a tow away zone."

Ennis shrugged it off, "We're an emergency vehicle. They can't tow us."

She begged to differ but by the time she began to protest, he'd already exited the car. Savannah left the red bubble light rotating on the dash to at least give the impression the unmarked sedan was official. She held off lecturing Ennis too hard, settling for, "They must be delightfully courteous in Texas, especially at Christmas."

"Why do you say that?"

"Because in the rat race known as Christmas in Atlanta, it's everyone for themselves. You'd be safer running with the bulls in Pamplona. They're gonna tow our car because we're blocking traffic." She directed his attention to their detective's car that shrunk the lane of traffic to one instead of two. Minutes earlier cars moved slow but steadily both ways. Now the congestion piled up for a quarter mile. Drivers were forced to take turns maneuvering around their Ford and, as usual, tempers flared in the process.

Savannah winced at the honking horns. She looked to her partner and husband. Ennis's shoulders drooped, "I'm too damn tired to move the car. We won't be in there long." He turned to walk off.

She smirked, "That's what you think."

Built in 1959, Lenox Square Mall was the largest shopping center South of New York at the time. Back then it housed two department stores, Davison's and Rich's, and boasted a lofty 60 specialty shops, a bowling alley, movie theater and grocery store. The slogan at the time was "Everything's there at Lenox Square". More than forty years later, it ballooned to three anchor stores – Bloomingdale's, Neiman Marcus and Macy's – and had over 250 specialty stores including Cartier, Brooks

Brothers and Louis Vuitton. The theater was still around and plenty more restaurants and eateries burgeoned the mall into a buzzing mini-metropolis. Many times Savannah thought they ought to redo the slogan to say "More than everything's there at Lenox Square."

If their suspect managed to escape, finding him in Lenox Square Mall was worse than picking through a haystack for a needle. This particular needle would be lost in basically a four story haystack with the current population of a small country. Four levels, over 250 stores, and God only knew how many restrooms and guest service kiosks there were. If he made it outside, yet another Atlanta nightmare awaited them. Holiday traffic with horsepower behind it. Savannah cringed at the mere idea this guy might slip through their fingers.

The two trudged into the masses that allotted a slim twelve inches between each human. Both Savannah and Ennis pulled their elbows close to their side arms to protect them. In that mass of humanity, billfolds easily lifted from pockets and purses easily slid from even the firmest grasp. Crooks found such crowds alluring. They stole and disappeared into the throng before anyone could reach them, much less retrieve the stolen goods, so the two detectives protected their holstered guns with extra vigilance.

They passed something called "The Art of Shaving" which Ennis thought amusing. Savannah could barely keep her wits about her with all the bustle of people. Her claustrophobia kicked into high gear upon sight of the mall parking lot. They kept walking, their progress slow. By the time they passed Davante, Ennis's sense of humor darkened to just about her shade. At The Tinder Box, they both felt the name's impact, considering this assignment should have been given to a uniform cop, not two detectives.

After several minutes of arduous walking and battling their way to center court, they spied the man they sought. Santa. The mall set up an elaborate "Elf Land" for Kris Kringle, including a Santa house flanked by giant candy canes and snowmen. White fluffy batting served as snow and blanketed both sides of the walkway until reaching a little house with a traditionally generous Southern porch. Sitting in a large gold throne-like chair sat a man posing as Santa.

The red velvet rope draped along golden posts intended to corral the enthusiastic children into a line. Tonight though, the rope didn't help anyone do anything except get in the way. Kids surrounded the little picket fence, its gatekeeper a short, chubby man dressed as an elf. After a second glance, Savannah decided by his features and mannerisms he fit better with the Sopranos more than with Santa. His pasted on smile for the kiddies darkened to a lascivious grin when his vision met Savannah's. She hoped for the elf's sake he wiped it from his face before Ennis saw it. Her new husband highly disapproved of other men's advances toward her or their disrespecting her and Ennis didn't mind showing them either.

She stood in a sea of shining little faces, their mouths poised into many type smiles. Gleeful, apologetic, mischievous and even some scared smiles. The kids were eager to push past her to see the Big Man. They'd waited all year for this. Now they stood mere yards from him, the wait only minutes, not months.

Savannah and Ennis studied Santa from afar. They watched him "ho ho ho" his way through another tyke's Most Wanted list and watched him lend a helping hand to the next child climbing into his broad lap. He was good, Savannah admitted that but not quite savvy enough to fool one perceptive mother. The mother called the police after Santa asked for the little girl's address and kindly inquired if they had an alarm system. "Santa needs to know so he doesn't wake good little children when he delivers their gifts," he'd said.

Yeah right, Savannah thought. *More like removing gifts for himself...* Why else would the counterfeit Mr. Claus set up shop in Lenox Square Mall, one of the richest in Atlanta?

"Should we shake him down in front of all these kids?" Ennis asked.

Savannah angled her vision to her partner. He scanned the crowd apprehensively, as though towing Santa away in handcuffs made him slightly ill. The image encouraged her to pause as well. Not a sweet vision. In fact, her brain concocted all sorts of scenarios, the foremost being a kindergarten riot, complete with television cameras filming the mugging of Santa by two Atlanta police detectives. Savannah could see the headlines in the Journal-Constitution: "Santa assaulted by Atlanta's Not-So-Finest."

She shook her head, "How did we draw the short straw tonight?"

"We asked for Christmas off. I think that rolled us into the purgatory bin."

Nodding grimly, she agreed, "We get to bust the bogus Santa while two uniforms get to search for the real one." She noticed his mouth tilted into a half smile, "Ennis, you *know* what I meant."

"How're we gonna do this without drowning in a tidal wave of kid hell?"

"Let's try approaching him calmly and quietly." She'd already begun the hike through the children when she heard Ennis shout over the din of excited young voices, "Calm and quiet – that oughta work fine!"

Together they wound through the maze of tiny kids. Once at the front of the line, they were stopped by Lecherous Elf. Ennis restrained a smirk at the sight of the hefty man in a green suit accentuated by a green hat with jingle bells along the base and shoes that curled at the toes. Savannah figured it was more the red tights that tickled his funny bone. The elf resembled a stuffed turkey.

Trying to erase the image from her mind, Savannah told him, "We're here to see Santa."

"Ain't everyone? Stand in line, sweetheart." His eyes roamed her from head to toe, "He's gonna like having you on his lap."

The man's ravenous gaze was enough to spur Ennis's temper. Ever since she and Ennis met he'd protected her from chauvinistic comments or behavior. Since their marriage, however, he took safeguarding her to new heights. She finally learned to just accept it instead of scolding him. Today was a classic example of her stepping back to let her husband take over. He displayed his badge squarely in front of the elf's nose, "Listen, Elfboy. We're here to see Santa now, if you get my drift."

The man's eyes widened upon Savannah producing a twin to Ennis's badge. He took a step backward. Ennis tromped onto the fake, fluffy snow and swung the small white gate open to allow his partner through. He addressed the elf once again, "Good to know my Texas accent isn't too perplexing around these parts. Don't go too far. We may have some questions for you."

Approaching the fat man in the red suit, Savannah noticed his attention still riveted on the small child stating his Christmas list item by item using his fingers to check off each gift. Santa's patience wore thin on the seventh item, "I got the list, Tommy. I'll have it all there for you, 'kay?" He glanced up to catch Savannah discreetly revealing the badge clipped to her belt.

"It's gotta be blue, Santa, not the red one," the boy continued, not making a move to vacate the man's lap.

Santa looked mighty anxious, Savannah thought. His gloved hands cinched around the boy's waist to urge him down, "Red, not blue, got it."

As his feet hit the floor, the little boy frantically corrected, "No, *blue*! I want blue!"

"Whatever, kid. I'll get it there." Santa suddenly stood up, addressing the crowd, "Santa's gotta go." A resounding groan rose from the hundred or so kids. The parents crossed their arms, giving the man a look to wither even the strongest human.

Santa watched Savannah and Ennis close in and shuffled toward the edge of the "Santa House", feeling the need to expound on his sudden departure, "He's going back to the North Pole to get all your toys. See ya!" He bolted from the Lilliputian house, his booted feet bicycling through the deep snow batting carpeting Elf Land. He braced himself on the gingerbread lattice side of the house and gave a quick glimpse behind him. Savannah and Ennis were close behind. Throwing them a narrow frown, he yanked a giant candy cane down as he passed it, knocking it down to block their path. Both detectives hurdled it without any trouble. "Yeah, calmly and quietly," Ennis reminded her. "Great idea."

"Shut up and run," Savannah grumbled and jumped another candy cane Santa threw their way. "Okay, you. You can stop now or, if you keep running, you'll just go to jail tired."

In response, Santa picked up the pace through the cottony snow. Even in his ill fitting boots and clearly padded paunch, he easily hopped the small picket fence surrounding Elf Land but not before felling a giant eight foot snowman in the path. Both Savannah and Ennis locked on the brakes, backpedaling. Their feet slid from under them and they plopped on their backsides in the billowing snow. Ennis was first to gain his footing. He extended his hand to her, "That went well."

Savannah came to her feet with his help and they resumed their chase. Catching up with him took virtually no effort on their part. Several kids surrounded him, clinging to him while rattling off their "must have" lists. He tried to shake loose from their hold but found eager children stick like Velcro. There were five kids anchored to his arms and coat when Savannah snapped a handcuff on his left wrist, "You're coming with us."

With those normally benign words, she detected a change in the children's attitude. All their faces went from gleeful to grim in a heartbeat. When they heard Ennis reciting the Miranda Rights then saw Savannah snap Santa's right wrist in the other cuff, she could have sworn every child turned icy. Ennis noticed the change as well, "Didn't they make a movie about this?"

Cutting her vision to Ennis, she whispered, "Yeah. 'Children of the Corn.'"

With the exception of a baby crying somewhere in the crowd, the whole center court fell deathly quiet. The small, stunned faces now evolved to anger. Ennis cleared his throat uneasily, "Let's get him outta here before they sprout claws…"

"Kids!" Santa yelled, startling both detectives. "They're taking Santa to jail!"

The announcement equated to a proclamation of war. Several kids, none older than nine and many of the older siblings of the now bawling youngsters, let out a rebel yell and lit out toward the two cops. Seeing the older children's bold move, a hoard of younger kids decided to charge while screaming like miniature banshees. Savannah and Ennis watched a literal tsunami of youth roll toward them. "Free Santa!" a sea of screaming voices chanted. "Free Santa!"

Savannah pulled on Santa's arm, her anger more than palpable, "Oh, thanks for being so helpful. Say another word and I'll shove a handful of snow in your mouth."

"Police brutality!" he squawked as she lead him along, his feet dragging to delay the inevitable. His cry, though, produced the intended effect… The kids swarmed like bees.

Kids of varying ages wrapped themselves around Savannah's legs, pulling her back with all their might. Trying to hoist a leg for two inches of progress became arduous with forty pounds of kid hanging onto the extremity. "Let go, you little brats," she growled in her nicest voice, which come to think of it, wasn't very nice at all. Still, it wasn't enough to budge the protestors. They clung like bears on a tree trunk, their tiny fingers digging into the flesh when they gripped. Oh, she hated to see the bruises those little hands would create.

She looked over to Ennis for some help and found him just as disabled as she – with the exception that four kids had him by the legs, not two like her. "Where are your mommies and daddies?" she heard him addressing the hangers-on. "Once we get this fella in jail, your parents are next! Then we'll take you little angels to –"

"Ennis," she broke his impending declaration. Child Protective Services was next from his lips and Savannah knew they were in enough poo to last a long time. They didn't need irate parents in their faces asking why their children were promised a permanent vacation from them.

"Well, God sakes, what else is gonna get these mangy things off us?"

She was about to open her mouth when a considerable pain registered at the back of her head. Some kid had her by the ponytail now and yanked on it like he jockeyed a racehorse. With every pull the pain grew in intensity. He yanked once, twice, three times and she rounded on the kid, "Okay, that does it." She grabbed him around the waist only to have the kid slam his elbow into her. The youngster's aim managed to zero in on her left breast and the impact of his elbow brought a muted cry from her lips. Of course it would be the sorest part of her, she thought – and what infuriated her most was the kid friggin' smiled about it like he knew how much it hurt.

Her soft yelp focused Ennis's attention on her, "You okay?"

I hope so, she thought to herself but replied, "Yeah, fine."

She tightened her hold around the kid's waist but before lifting him, a caution from her doctor rang an alarm in her brain. No heavy lifting, he'd said. She assumed a six or seven year-old qualified as heavy lifting, at least according to her physician. She grabbed the boy's wrist instead. "Who belongs to this?" she yelled over the crowd.

After a mere moment, a panicked mother weaved through the throng of kids to pluck her darling from Savannah's hold, "I'm sorry, Officer. I don't know what got into him. Gary's not a bad boy, he —"

"Just make sure he stays to himself. That's all I ask." She resisted the urge to cry as well as cradle her now throbbing breast. Normally it could withstand a thump like that without literally making her sick to her stomach. This time, however, Savannah swallowed back the heaving sensation creeping up her throat.

Gary's mother backed away, assuring Savannah he would then frowned at her boy, promising repercussions for his actions. Savannah highly doubted it. Parents rarely punished children these days, at least the way her mother punished her and her siblings. While R.J. equated beatings to punishment, Charlene believed in good old fashioned spankings. The kind that changed a child's mind about misbehavior, not the kind that left scars. Their mother was a disciplinarian but still a soft heart. She never took the punishment too far or let up before the lesson was well learned. Parents these days, Savannah shook her head, could learn a damn fine lesson from Charlene Prince. "Time outs" were crap tied with a bow. A kid never learned anything from one except how to manipulate the parents. A hickory limb applied to the offender's backside — now *that* made an impression. No, little Gary What's-His-Name would grow up to be just like their handcuffed Santa. Full of himself, full of disdain for authority and an eventual headache to law enforcement.

"What's on my back, a crab?" Ennis broke her train of thought. She glanced as he turned, revealing another kid, this one standing behind him, pinching his back in as many places as possible to inflict as much pain as Ennis could endure. Savannah had to hand it to the kid. He had a pair of mitts that looked darn near lethal for his age. So she swatted at him as best she could, telling him to leave Ennis alone.

Her partner hollered another cry when the kid wrung another piece out of him. Ennis didn't sound grateful for her efforts, if anything he sounded aggravated with them, "That *really* helped. He's not pinching *nearly* as hard now."

"Well, I could let him keep pinching ya. Would that make you–" her smart comeback ended in her own muted shriek as a tyke landed squarely on her back. His arms wrapped around neck and lodged against her windpipe and his knees clamped down on her hips as if she'd throw him like a bucking bull threw his rider. These kids meant business. Christmas Eve and all the kids had last minute concerns with Santa. And she and Ennis stood in their way. "Ennis," she croaked.

He stared right at her and cupped his hand around his ear, "I can't hear you. Did you need something specific?"

The smartass, she thought. Taking Christmas vacation wasn't her decision alone. As she recalled he was just as responsible for this chaotic mess as she, "I'll kill you myself if you don't get this kid off me," she warned.

Ennis let the kid ride her back another few seconds then fisted the kid's shirt in his hand to pull him free. Savannah felt the boy tighten his hold all over her. Every time Ennis pulled on him, his legs dug harder into her hips and his arms constricted on her throat. She felt her gun embossing its print on her hipbone. With her luck, the impression would last a month.

Ennis gave one last, genuine tug on the kid, "C'mon, you rug rat. Get off her."

"Make me," the boy taunted. "I want to see Santa. You ain't takin' him to jail."

Savannah braced herself. A person didn't dare Ennis and a person shouldn't ever taunt him, kids included. The boy bit off more than he could chew with Mr. Rutherford. He appreciated that fact in short order. Ennis let Santa go long enough to take the boy by the wrists. The death grip turning Savannah a nice shade of plum finally eased. Ennis peeled the top half of the kid away then leveled an ultimatum, "If you don't get off this police officer, I'll haul you, your parents and any other relatives to the slammer and as a bonus, I'll personally write the *real* Santa and tell him what a bad kid you are. You'll get squat for Christmas."

Savannah saw her partner demolish the boy with his best angered look, "Cops are number one in Santa's book. Know why? Because we give him escorts into every town. So he listens very carefully to us."

The little boy's eyes widened to saucers. Savannah felt his legs slacken until he slid to the floor. They watched him stand, arms crossed with frowning look of disbelief, "Whaddya mean the *real* Santa?"

Suddenly their immediate surroundings quieted down significantly. The boy's question perked the interest of every kid around them. Savannah's heart raced in her chest, the pounding echoing in her ears. She hated to even breathe for fear the action might incite another peewee riot. Instead of concentrating their efforts on annihilating the police, the gaggle of youths presently focused their attention at the man in the red suit.

Now the handcuffed Santa began to sweat beneath the beard and fake eyebrows. Looking closer, Savannah recognized the fear coursing behind his eyes. Santa planned on making a fast getaway. His diversion ultimately failed, forcing him to develop another escape route. On every criminal's list of last resort is "run". The instant his eyes met hers, Savannah grabbed his arm with one hand and rested her other on her holstered weapon, whispering, "Don't make me shoot you in front of all these kids. I promise you the wound won't be fatal. I can't promise you that these disappointed kids won't thump on you a while and I certainly wouldn't promise that the angry parents won't finish what my bullet started." She hadn't really meant she'd shoot him but he hadn't known it. Plus, she *had* meant she'd let the kids and parents waylay him a while, at least until she and Ennis meandered toward the tumble of arms and legs to separate them from Phony Santa.

"Yeah," another kid piped up, one that resembled a future wrestler. His cheeks blossomed to a rich scarlet much like the curly mop atop his head. His features tweaked with anger while his chubby hands rolled into balls. His problem, as his vision swung from them to Santa, was simply who to direct his ire toward, "Whaddya mean the real Santa?"

Savannah cleared her throat, "Well, this man isn't Santa. He's a fake."

"How do you know?" a small girl's voice called from within the crowd. The indignant tone sounded mixed heavily with sadness.

"It's quite simple," Savannah continued. Her voice gained the composure and confidence it lacked for several minutes. She had every child's attention now, "Santa knows every child's name. You." She waved her rider closer, "Ask him what your name is."

The imp that fastened himself onto her back gave her a narrow glare upon his approach. She lowered her brow in response, "Ask him."

Still riding on anger – at least not on her back – the kid crossed his arms and sucked in a deep breath, preparing himself. "What's my name?" he inquired flatly.

Phony Santa seared her with his own glare. Ennis joined the show, "Answer the kid."

Santa's face colored beneath the beard. He was crimson as his coat when he whispered to Savannah, "Just get me outta here."

"Not before you answer his question."

Ennis leaned in to offer hope, "If you get it right, we might let you go."

The man shot a new volley of visual arrows Ennis's direction. The boy tugged on the red velvet coat, "Hey, what's my name?"

"What's his name?" a few others chimed in, and before long, the whole mass chanted the question repeatedly.

Santa shifted his most pitiful expression to Savannah, "Please get me outta here. I'm beggin' ya."

"Tell him his name or tell him you don't know." Ennis said. "Then we'll go." A tugging on her slacks brought her attention downward. A golden haired girl, younger than Lindsey, glanced up with tears in her big blue eyes, "Don't take Santa," she pleaded.

Savannah's heart tugged harder at her than the little girl. Kids could always make you feel like a bona fide chump. Taking a deep breath, Savannah tried to concoct a reasonable excuse for handcuffing the man posing as Santa. Handing him off to Ennis's custody, she crouched down to eye level with the girl, "Don't cry, sweetheart. This man isn't Santa, he's only dressed like him. We're going to find the real Santa for you. Then you can tell him what you want for Christmas."

The tears gradually slowed. The girl seemed to soak up each word, weighing its worth, then leaned to Savannah's ear, "If you see him, will you tell him to find our puppy?"

"Your puppy got lost?"

The little girl nodded, her lip puffed like she tuned up to cry, "It's my brother's puppy but I love her too. Her name is Paris."

Savannah swept a tear from the child's cheek, "If I see Santa, I'll tell him about Paris. What's your name, honey?"

The girl gave the fake Santa a disparaging glance then cupped her hands around the detective's ear, "Sarah."

"I'll tell him then when you see Santa, you can tell him too, okay, Sarah?" Normally, Savannah wasn't kid crazy. She preferred them stay to themselves and she'd do the same. The only exceptions: Lindsey and Dylan. Otherwise kids weren't her forte. But, as with life, some kids surprised her. Little Sarah with her golden hair and sad blue eyes pulled at more than her heart. She pulled at her biological clock. Besides her niece and nephew, this girl made her want to have kids. Common sense severed that idea though. She'd have to give up what she loved – being a detective, out on the streets interviewing, collecting evidence, and solving cases. Police work nearly completed her. Nearly. A daughter that looked to her with the admiration and love the way Lindsey looked to Leah would undoubtedly complete it. Even if she wanted kids, her current problem prevented the notion of having one in the near future.

"You okay down there?" Ennis inquired, his voice softening as if realizing it was a poignant moment for her.

"Yeah," Savannah blinked, surprised to discover tears trembling in her eyes. She swiped them away with her thumbs. She hated showing emotion in public and in front of Ennis.

She surveyed the crowd, seeing too many adults gathering closer and none looking panicked that their daughter was out of sight. "Do you see your mama or daddy, honey?"

Sarah pointed behind them. Savannah turned and saw a woman approaching, summoning the girl by her name, "I'm sorry she's bothering you, Officer."

"She's not a bother at all. She wanted me to tell Santa that Paris is lost and she wants her back."

The mother smiled kindly, "Oh, Paris. Sarah is partial to her even though the dog is my son's." She rolled her eyes, "He named her after Paris Hilton of all people."

No wonder the dog ran away, Savannah thought. She returned the smile with a lifted brow, "Some things are without explanation." Brushing another tear from Sarah's cheek, she finished, "You stay close to Mama, okay? I don't want you getting lost too."

The girl nodded, leaned into her mother's hold. The sight coerced the fake Santa to own up, "Geez, this is killin' me. I don't know the kid's name, alright? Just get me outta here."

Savannah rose, turned to the red-suited imposter with a look threatening serious bodily harm, "Where'd you stash Santa, you creep?"

He jerked his head to the right, "He's in the men's restroom."

She reached in her suit jacket for the walkie-talkie, "You guys still on the plaza level?"

A brief silence ensued then a voice answered, "Yeah. Why, you got something?"

"Santa's impersonator. The real deal is in the men's restroom on the mall level. Would you get him and bring him back here so these kids don't mutiny on us again?"

A laugh sprang from the speaker, "Whatsa matter, Detective? You and Rutherford can't handle crowd control anymore?"

Savannah leveled a baleful glare at the walkie-talkie. The fake Santa laughed out loud which set her on edge, "You shut up. You're takin' a ride anyway." Debating on whether to volley back a response, she finally settled on, "Remind me again, Jeffries, when were you trying for that promotion?"

"Copy that, Detective. We're on our way to rescue the fat man."

She and Ennis attempted to wade through the throng of kids and parents only to be detained yet again. They all closed in, asking questions, demanding answers. Ennis finally had enough, "Everyone pipe down! Officers will soon be escorting the real Santa to his," he hesitated while searching for the right word, "his..."

"House at Elf Land," Savannah prompted.

"His house at Elf Land where you can all place your Christmas orders with him. Be nice to him, he's had a hard night already." He turned to his handcuffed companion, "As for you, we have a special room reserved for people like you."

They wound their way through the massive crowds at Lenox Square Mall until reaching the parking lot – which stood strangely empty of their detective's car. Ennis searched the immediate area for it, "What the hell…"

"I told you not to park there. A tow away zone means just that on Christmas."

"But we're cops. They can't just take off with our car."

"They did take off with it."

The imposter glanced hesitantly at Ennis then Savannah, "You're not gonna make me walk to jail, are you?"

"We should but that means we'd have to also," she said. Then an idea struck her. Visually scanning the parking lot, she ultimately spied the squad car parked near the front of a row. Ennis followed her line of vision, a grin spread on his face, "Do you want to tell 'em or should I?"

"You do it. If Jeffries says one more silly word to me, I'm liable to smack him."

2

"How's your..." Ennis began without obviously knowing how to phrase it tastefully, especially with a suspect in the car. "Where that kid hit you?"

Savannah grimaced again. The pain ebbed into a general ache that refused to be ignored. She didn't touch it for fear of waking a worse pain so she settled for staring at it occasionally. "Aches but I'll take something later for it."

"Did he hit you pretty hard?"

No, actually he hadn't. The kid's elbow grazed it sufficiently enough but any extra pressure – including her bra – caused it to hurt. She assumed Ennis wondered why she bowed out of their romantic evenings lately. She'd used fatigue from work as an excuse for a few days now. Fabricating a new, believable one might take a while so she made a mental note to start thinking about it. Since the biopsy, her breast ached on and off so the thought of romping – normally a pleasurable idea – caused a considerable flinch that week.

Her gut told her to enlighten Ennis about her doctor's appointment and biopsy. He'd hit the roof once he found out but

Savannah hated to worry him. He worried over her enough *without* a doctor's appointment and no time was a good time to tell him the week's events.

"You guys really pissed off those other cops," the imposter – whose name turned out to be Ricky Langsford – said.

"We did read him his rights, didn't we?" Savannah inquired from the passenger's seat.

Ennis nodded, "Every last one of them."

She twisted in the seat to address the suspect, "Then I suggest you heed them, especially the first one. Be quiet."

Ricky shrugged, "Not my ass that's in a crack. They sounded ready to rip you in half for taking their car."

Leaning closer to Ennis, she whispered, but not too covertly, "While we're on I-85, let me toss him out in traffic."

Playing along, her partner scolded, "Now, Detective, it's against the rules to exercise such liberties."

"*Please...*" she begged. "We can always claim he jumped."

The threat penetrated Ricky's brain and he backed off, "Okay, okay, I'll shut up." His backside burrowed further into the seat and he pouted, "Wouldn't surprise me if you tried it anyway."

"You keep flapping your gums and I'll do more than try," she warned.

The cruiser's radio crackled to life, "Sixteen twelve,"

Savannah reached for the mike, "Sixteen twelve, go ahead."

"Sixteen twel – Prince, is that you?"

Here it came: the barrage of jokes referring to losing detective's cars and swiping squad cars, "Affirmative."

"Why are you in a squad car?"

"Long story. I'll tell you when we get to the station. What's the call since we're here?"

The dispatcher relayed an address and the complaint of a domestic dispute. Savannah took note of the address, signed off and glanced at Ennis, "Incidentally, you get to explain about the car. I advised against parking in the tow away zone, if you remember."

Ennis rolled his eyes skyward, "After we answer this call, we'll get the cruiser back to the uniforms and call it a night."

"Y'know," Ricky offered, "you could get an earlier start on Christmas if you'd let me go. Look at it as a gift of sorts."

Savannah and Ennis looked at each other and nearly laughed. Their passenger correctly interpreted their expressions, "Hey, my mother's in a nursing home, okay? I promised to be there on Christmas."

She propped her elbow on the door and sighed, "First of all, you pried addresses out of those kids. Santa knows everyone's address, dummy, he doesn't have to ask. Second, if you don't remember, you fraudulently passed yourself off as Santa Claus who you conveniently stuffed in the men's bathroom at Lenox Square Mall. That itself should count as some degree of blasphemy. You tarnished the reputation of a well respected icon." She leaned her head against her hand, "There's got to be a special place in Hell for people like you."

"I'm sorry, okay? Can't we please forget this, just this once? My mother is expecting me tonight."

"You shouldn't have been up to no good," Ennis responded in a voice refusing argument. "Your mama'd be ashamed of you and you know it."

Temporarily defeated, Ricky remained silent for several seconds. Then he mumbled, "Those cops are gonna kill you for taking the car."

Savannah frowned into the back seat, "Ennis, drive really fast on I-85. We'll see if Santa bounces."

The cruiser's headlights cut through the curtain of night as they approached their next call. The dispatcher's description of the problem put both detectives on edge. A domestic disturbance sounded straightforward. In reality it spelled nightmare a thousand different ways. Yelling, beating, stabbing, shooting and many times it was all heaped on the responding officers for interrupting the whole mess.

They turned onto Wrightsboro Drive, the location of the disturbance, and Ennis started his usual speech, "If things get rough, call for back-up from the car."

She wondered how long he'd wait before saying it. At the slightest hint of impending danger, she was instructed to stay behind and call for back-up. There were times she realized why they didn't let married couples partner up on the job. "Ennis, you can call for back-up just as easily as I can."

A chuckle rose from the back seat, "Equal opportunity, man."

Ennis glared at the rearview mirror, "Shut up back there." He crept down the street and while checking house numbers he continued his lecture, "Just listen to me this one time, okay?"

Savannah reached in her suit jacket to withdraw her answer, "That's why God invented the portable radio. I can still back you up and call for reinforcements." She pointed ahead, "Five doors up on the right."

Most homes in the area didn't have yard or porch lights but thankfully the area wasn't prone to too much violence, just calls on loud music or a "domestic disturbance" or two…

As they approached, they saw people lining the sidewalks and others emerging from their homes. All congregated to one large gathering of gawkers spilling into the street.

Ennis pulled to the curb, right behind an older model sedan parked halfway on the curb. Savannah remembered the unique parking stance from her childhood. After her father finished his daily round of drinking, he'd find his way home and half-ass park his pickup out front, narrowly missing her mother's prized magnolia tree.

The sedan suffered much the same plight. Its front end managed to hit the asphalt while the rear end, the right rear tire balanced precariously on the curb's edge, was aimed skyward with the trunk yawning open. The contents struck the two detectives speechless. A giant plastic snowman jutted out sideways like a half-felled tree, its huge grin aimed straight at them.

"What the hell is going on here?" Ennis asked.

Savannah looked out the passenger side window to witness another bizarre scene, "I'm not sure but the show's over to the right."

Multicolored lights lined the roof's apex and hung along the porch of the modest little house. They winked on and off in an alternating sequence of orange, blue, red, green and white.

Atop the roof sat a brown plastic reindeer and Santa not unlike the snowman wedged into the trunk. With such a small house Savannah wondered where the occupant stored such humongous decorations throughout the year, considering the snowman's girth measured around three feet wide.

Watching the action on the roof, she could understand why the police were summoned. Besides witnessing a full grown man trying to wrestle the giant plastic Santa from the roof, that full grown male was also naked as the day of his birth except for a pair of shoes. His body, big and doughy, wasn't quite doughy enough to hide the credentials below his navel.

He grappled with Santa in a wild, perverse battle that she expected to see on Pay-Per-View or the internet later that night. Frustrated that the plastic decoration wasn't giving up the fight easily, the man got his revenge by flouncing around, stomping Christmas lights along the peak of the roof.

"We gotta fix this quick," Savannah said, opening her door. "Kids are watching."

Ennis followed suit but not before putting Ricky on notice, "You leave this car and I *will* let her drop you on the freeway."

Ennis approached the house while Savannah addressed the neighbors, "Go back inside and for God's sake, take your kids with you. In case you haven't noticed, this isn't the Disney Channel." She stood, arms crossed, until every curious soul disappeared inside their homes then she headed across the street to join her partner. The closer she got, she heard a woman's voice ramp up from generally annoyed to virtually hysterical, "Stop ruinin' my display, Hank! You said I could have 'em!"

Savannah hurried faster. When the yelling started, the beating or shooting followed close behind and she didn't want Ennis fending off two enraged people by himself. As she approached, she tried to hide a smile. With her fiery red hair styled into a beehive, the lanky loudmouth reminded her of Flo from the old TV show "Alice". If the words "Hank, kiss my grits!" fell from her lips, Savannah wouldn't have been surprised, she'd have rolled on the lawn laughing her ass off.

Ennis introduced himself and his partner but the woman ignored his presence until she screamed a brief but descriptive expletive at Hank. Momentarily satisfied, she turned to Ennis, "'Bout damn time you got here. I called ya twenty minutes ago. Can y'all get his ass down 'fore he destroys my decorations?"

Ennis reached in his suit jacket for pen and paper then decided against it, "Who is he?"

"My ex-husband. The dumb son of a bitch wants my Christmas lights and I specifically asked for 'em in the divorce. I got 'em now he's up there stompin' 'em to dust. Won't be nothin' left by the time you people decide to stop him."

A swell of temper rose to the surface. Citizens never quite grasped a cop's life during the Christmas season. Between traffic accidents caused by impatient drivers and physical altercations in crowded parking lots, officers also juggled domestic disputes which, for the record, tipped the scale at Christmas. Savannah's head ached at the remembrance of her uniform days. People turned vicious at the time of year they also preached love, tolerance and peace. None of which police ever experienced until well into January if they were lucky.

Before allowing her temper to spark, Savannah strolled to the front yard. If Ennis kept the wife busy disparaging law enforcement, she'd try to talk The Streak down. Savannah held her badge much like Van Helsing warding off Dracula, "Sir, climb down from the roof now."

He either didn't hear her or pretended not to. He continued rampaging across the roof, a raised knee followed shortly by a popping sound. Savannah visually scanned the sidewalks for snoopy neighbors. At least they had the sense not to poke their heads outside but a few curtains parted in houses across the way.

Oblivious to the attention he'd drawn, Hank methodically crunched each bulb along the string. Savannah cupped her hands around her mouth, "Sir, I'm with the police. Climb down now before you hurt yourself." *Or I get pissed and help you down myself.* She rethought that. With so many onlookers, the best tactic would be calling for back-up. Let the uniforms crawl up there and bring him down. Since Hank was obviously sloshed, she'd hold off calling for back-up. Chances were, he'd lose his balance and roll off the roof in the hedgerow below.

He glanced down, squinting at her badge, "Police you say?"

"Yes. Come down from the roof. We need to talk to you."

He stood as if contemplating the order. She sensed somewhere in his pickled brain he'd misunderstood what she said because he turned to face her in all his nude glory and displayed his middle finger, "Forget it. That bitch ain't gettin' my lights. I bought 'em, they're mine." His foot swung back and kicked the reindeer over, sending it skidding down the roof.

"Savannah, watch out!" Ennis yelled.

Thankfully she already saw the runaway reindeer and side-stepped it. It fell unceremoniously to the grass, landing face up, its ridiculous grin smiling up at her. She lifted her vision from it to the naked man on the roof. Her voice revealed her growing anger, "*Get down here* or I'll find the meanest cops on the job to help you down."

By that time, Ennis rushed beside her, realizing the danger the drunk posed. He urged her back, took off his suit jacket and handed it to her.

"What are you doing?" She asked the question like he'd announced he could fly.

"I'll get the bastard down myself. You coulda been killed."

Highly doubtful, she thought to herself. Maybe a knot on the head or a bruise here and there but plastic reindeer weren't prominently known to kill. She put a hand to his arm, "Wrestling with a drunk on a roof poses more likelihood of death than being conked by a plastic Rudolph. The guy's got hundred proof breath."

"You get down here before I come after you!" Ennis boomed and jolted Savannah so bad she herself nearly backed off a step.

The boisterous command also startled Hank. Savannah saw him sway and she urged Ennis back a ways. Thanks to the alcohol, Hank's legs wobbled to and fro and his arms pinwheeled in a vain attempt to retain his balance. Fear rounded his eyes and for safety's sake, Savannah pulled her husband aside, clearing the way in case Hank tumbled.

Hank tipped forward until sprawled flat on his belly, his weight and pitch of the roof expediting his speedy descent toward the house's overhang. Sympathy pains shivered their way down Savannah's spine. Hank's chest and parts south were suffering road rash as he slid down the rough composition shingles.

Hank released a yell resembling a bleating goat. Oddly, Hank slid like Rudolph had moments earlier, only the former landed in the hedge and not on the grass as the latter.

A distinct groaning emerged from the bushes. They shimmied and swayed violently as he thrashed about. Savannah feared he'd pop out from behind the hedges like a prairie dog from its hole. "Stay behind that hedge," Savannah ordered, "until we cover you with something."

"Lady," he whimpered, "there ain't nothin' left to cover."

She bent closer and, in a tone that prohibited disagreement, warned, "You stay behind that bush or I'll make that trip down the roof look like a day at the spa. I'll call an ambulance for you but only if you stay put."

After muttering a string of expletives powerful enough to stun even the heartiest of sailors, Hank uttered a reference to not wanting an ambulance.

Ennis clicked on his flashlight, leaned over the hedge. Savannah saw the beam sweep behind the bushes then stop. In the subdued light, she saw her husband wince, "Call one anyway," he said. "May not be life-threatening but he sure ain't gonna wear shorts anytime soon."

3

Exasperating and futile. Savannah recalled those particular terms about her uniform days. For every hundred calls, perhaps ten fell into the "that's why I became a cop" category. Sitting outside Flo's house while another radio car whisked their fake Santa to jail, she considered her life as a uniform officer and not a detective. The picture depressed her.

They both spoke to Hank's ex-wife about dropping the trespass and vandalism charges. In the beginning, she mulled it over but not too heavily. Once they explained she'd have to appear in court, she bowed out, "Not if I'm gonna miss my stories. I got one where a girl's stuck under a bus. Another's about to give birth but she don't know that the father's really the mayor's long lost son who's also got a paternal twin that's causing all sorts of hell."

Savannah resisted the urge to correct her. Ennis didn't, "You mean fraternal twin."

One of Flo's flaming red brows hiked up an inch, "No, these are paternal. They don't look a thing alike. You must be watching a different story."

"So you're not filing charges on Hank," Savannah redirected the conversation back.

"No point. The bastard won't be able to steal my decorations now," she bragged. "He got taught a good lesson."

"Yes, ma'am, and quite a painful one," Savannah agreed without the same enthusiasm. Somehow the woman derived too much pleasure from the image for Savannah's taste. Divorces were ugly things but the bitterness they created was far worse. The thought made her grateful for Dane. He kept Georgia buoyed through the divorce from Matthew. When Dane wasn't visiting, he was calling. To see her sister genuinely smile again was the best Christmas gift of all.

She and Ennis retreated to the cruiser, and Savannah uttered a silent prayer the city quieted down long enough for them to radio the unit out of service. The ache in her breast started in earnest now and a painkiller sounded mighty tempting.

They'd wrestled Hank from the bowels of the boxwoods only for him to reward them with a good old fashioned fight. Between the detectives, two uniform officers and the paramedics, they finally loaded him into the ambulance but not before her pain made a serious resurgence.

"What's wrong?" Ennis asked.

She cringed, rolled her shoulder but managed only to inflame the ache, "I'm hurting a little."

"Take something for it."

That was easier said than done, "I can't until we're off duty." On second thought, it might be easier than originally thought, "How about calling it a night?"

He sighed from the driver's seat, "You've got my vote. All this holiday spirit will drive a person to suicide. Let's head home before we're as jolly as they are."

Ennis echoed a sentiment she believed for years. Despite being a joyous time of year for some people, Christmas was also a stressful time. Suicides rose sharply in December and Savannah always wondered what drove each person to such drastic measures. A death in the family? A bitter divorce like Hank and his wife? Being alone for the holidays? Credit card bills or foreclosure on a house? Being diagnosed with a terminal disease?

She shut out the depressing thoughts but the effort it took disheartened her all over again. Keeping herself buoyed grew harder with her personal struggle and the fact her job didn't exactly promote Christmas cheer. Cops saw dreadful situations all year. Christmas should be sacred but no one seemed to care. The meaner the better, as evidenced by the burglary rate skyrocketing at that time of year. Assaults and murders rose to summertime levels, an anomalous spike in a twelve month year. Cops knew what it was. EMTs and firefighters did too. People couldn't handle holiday stress so they lost their marbles – and accused someone else of stealing them.

She released her hair from the ponytail and ran a hand through the waves to loosen them. Ennis held a particular fancy for her dark, unruly tresses. She hadn't a clue why but when she glanced over, she caught him bobbing his brow at her. She couldn't help but smile, "Stop getting ideas. They probably installed cameras in here to record our every move."

"Sugar," he boasted, "with our passion, we'd melt the lenses." He eased the car into a leisure pace then proceeded to dial a number on his cell, "I'll check our messages at home. I'm expecting Ma will probably call and wish us a Merry Christmas."

She nodded in response. Traffic still presented a nightmare as cars sped through intersections only to tap their brakes upon sight of the cruiser. The detectives had no intention of stopping anyone unless absolutely necessary. At least drivers *tried* to behave when presented with the threat. In Christmases past, drivers literally sped all the way home with her on their tails, the cruiser lights flashing and siren wailing. Those drivers received an extra special present that Christmas called a trip to jail.

From the corner of her eye, she saw Ennis punch in the key code with his thumb. He listened then smiled, "We're popular. Got three messages."

The approaching light blinked red and he slowed to a stop. Savannah took the opportunity to check her cell phone. She had no voicemails waiting. The fact gave her pause, her mood darkening. So much for the promise to call by seven on Christmas Eve... The guy wasn't merely fashionably late, he now officially topped her shit list.

Savannah glanced at the light which conveniently remained red then sensed her husband staring at her. Without meeting his gaze, she asked, "Did your mother call?"

"She called and so did Georgia but it's the third message I really want you to hear," his thumb stabbed another button then punched on the speakerphone.

Curious about his sudden dramatic nature – not to mention the brutal treatment of his phone – Savannah shifted her vision toward him. His mood wavered between uneasy puzzlement and cautious anger. She soon discovered why.

"This is Desmond Collier, Attorney at Law an' this message is for Savannah," a heavily accented voice announced from Ennis's phone. The thick Georgia brogue probably stumped her partner as the name Collier emerged "Collyah" and he managed to jumble "Attorney at Law" into a soup only a native Georgian could successfully decipher. The message proceeded in such fashion Savannah prayed Ennis felt more confusion than ire. While listening to Desmond speak, she busied herself decoding his words into English, "The papers are ready for your signature anytime. I'll be back in the office on Tuesday…"

She gripped the portable radio wishing it was Desmond's thick, fleshy neck. *That dumb shit*, she seethed. She specifically told Desmond not to call the house. That's why she gave him her *cell number* and the friggin' rat, like all lawyers, did what came naturally – he screwed things up worse. Now there were two men on her list. Desmond and the one man she desperately needed to hear from before Christmas Eve was a memory.

The cruiser suddenly bucked forward, shot through the intersection then screeched to a stop in a nearby parking lot. Ennis threw the gearshift into Park, jammed his phone back on his belt then pointedly turned to her, "Why'd you hire an attorney? Are we getting a divorce and I'm the last to find out?"

"You know better than that." The words sounded kinder than she expected. Their marriage a few months earlier not only settled her but blessed her with happiness she never experienced before. For Ennis to leap off the deep end and suggest otherwise nearly broke her calm exterior, not to mention her heart.

"Maybe I do but being blindsided by a lawyer isn't a cozy feeling. Savannah, what's going on?"

And this was exactly what she'd hoped to avoid – the invasive questions. The past week served nothing but hell and in a grand moment of stupidity, she decided Ennis needed protecting from it. She never planned to keep him in the dark forever – just long enough to sort out whatever life presented. Now that Ennis knew about Desmond, he'd dog her until she spilled every detail. Savannah braced herself. No amount of nagging could drag the truth from her until she wanted it dragged out. She tried to beg some peace from him, "Ennis, please."

Anger laced his voice, "Tell me why you need a damn lawyer. We're married, for God's sake. We don't keep secrets from each other." When she didn't confirm the fact, he added, "Do we?"

Normally, no, they didn't but growing up with an abusive father hardly promoted candidness. It encouraged just the opposite. Keep quiet and you might not get hurt. The older she got, the concept evolved to keep quiet and you might not hurt anyone else. By her lie of omission, she tried to save Ennis the anxiety weighing her down but as usual, she made him mad instead.

Ennis cussed a string of obscenities that might have impressed Naked Hank. He rummaged his suit coat pocket. "Here," he said then tossed a cellophane wrapped mystery at her. "Eat this."

She caught it in midair as he switched on the dome light. "A Twinkie?" She couldn't believe her eyes, "You keep Twinkies in your coat?"

"Never know how long a shift might last. Don't worry, I carry enough for us both." He opened his own cream-filled cake. One bite into it, he motioned for her to follow suit. By his stern features and tone, she felt like a kid being scolded to eat her broccoli or go to bed hungry.

The cellophane crackled as she peeled the wrapper open and took a bite. An unexpected urge to retch bolted up her throat at the first taste of the sweet creamy filling. She waited to chew then carefully ventured ahead with the task and prayed the stuff didn't bounce right back up.

She bit off another small portion of the sponge cake. So far so good. She was thankful Ennis partook of the snack too and hoped chewing on the Twinkie might lessen his desire to chew on her.

"Now, tell me what's going on."

Well, so much for keeping him quiet... She sighed then swallowed, "I'd rather wait to say."

"I'd rather you quit stalling and tell me what's wrong."

Savannah turned away, took another bite. The cream-filled yellow sponge cake was simply a means to an end. If her stomach agreed to hold it down, the painkiller came next, followed shortly by welcome relief. Guilt, not just pain, bore down on her conscience, making chewing abnormally difficult.

He would understand and support her every way possible through the waiting and ultimate outcome. She forced herself to swallow despite the mouthful being only half chewed.

"That kid musta put a hurtin' on you," her husband's voice softened which only brought her emotions floating closer to the surface. She nodded without speaking. Savannah stared through the tears trembling in her eyes. Ennis was gentle, thoughtful. She didn't deserve a man like him and she debated for days about telling him. In the end, she hadn't the heart to burden him with the news.

"Savannah." His hand covered hers, the tender squeeze pushed her to the brink of crying.

"I'll tell you later." She sat the remainder of her Twinkie on the dash then rifled her jacket for the pain pills. After chasing one down with a healthy swallow of Coke they bought earlier that evening, she sighed with hope that relief was minutes away. Sweeping away tears, she bolstered her courage to face Ennis. When she did, she found herself leaning away from her husband due to his withering scowl.

"You'll tell me now, damn it." His hands bunched into fists, "You're in tears."

Her mouth opened to respond. Ennis wagged a finger at her, "Don't say it. I know there's something wrong."

Movement from the corner of her eye drew her attention to two Christmas shoppers ambling down the sidewalk in front of the car. They halted at the raised voice, hesitantly glanced in their direction. Savannah saw their wide eyes swing between the large, well-muscled driver and the passenger who currently displayed about the same level of alarm they did. She shrank down in the seat to escape their invasive stares. From a civilian's point of view, she could only imagine how the scene might be interpreted – a male cop not only bawling out his female counterpart but slicing and dicing her in the process.

Oblivious to the extra eyes and ears, Ennis went on, "You've held me off in bed with a variety of excuses *then* I hear you've hired a lawyer for some inexplicable reason and *now* you're crying because you're hurting. If you don't tell me –"

"Sixteen twelve," the radio squawked.

Savannah instinctively recoiled as Ennis's large hand raced to the mike. In his frustration, he blurted, "Sixteen twelve is out of service," then slammed the mike onto the seat between them. He swiveled, his mighty form engulfing the driver's seat. His posture gave her pause but his words convinced her he meant business, "Savannah, tell me what's up or I swear I'll shake it outta you."

Hearing the threat delivered with the weight of a one ton anvil, the passers-by elected to move on.

Savannah swallowed uneasily. She wasn't particularly scared of Ennis but her mild-mannered husband concealed a pretty vicious temper. She never worried that he'd manhandle her or hit her – that was her father's bailiwick. However Ennis's present actions and mood informed he *would* shake the truth from her and make it memorable.

Despite her best efforts, the tears resurfaced, "Desmond isn't a divorce lawyer. He's an estate lawyer. He wrote my will."

Ennis's temper deflated like a pricked balloon, "A will? Why the hell do you need a will?"

"Well," she compelled her voice to remain halfway steady, "considering our line of work, I thought it was appropriate."

"Number one, that's bullshit unless you're planning to step in front of a bullet. Number two, why didn't we go to Collier together if that's why you needed a will? Why did you do this by yourself?"

"I wanted one, okay? And I didn't want you to find out until I was ready. I wanted you taken care of when I died. It worries me." And it had. It nagged at her during the day and hounded her worse at night when he slept beside her oblivious to her current situation.

Ennis reacted as if she'd spoken fluent Swahili, "I'm sorry, did I miss something important? *When* you die? Is this imminent and I slept through the newsflash?"

She averted her gaze. She saw his confusion melt into concern but also a generous amount of hurt sprinkled in the muddle of emotion. Above all, his anger still boiled hot on the surface and she couldn't bear to see any of it. If she faced him, she'd spill everything, the discovery, the biopsy and her fears.

His heated stare made her feel like a suspect being prodded into a confession. He'd perfected it and yes, it nearly worked. Nearly… "The papers should be straightforward as to who gets what. I want Lindsey to have some of Mama's things and I'm leaving you the house, my part of the orchards and –"

"Thanks," he butted in, "but I'd rather have you." He leaned in, closed the space between them. Ennis wasn't stupid. He remembered how Seth and Georgia interrogated her. They robbed her of space to move, to mentally breathe.

Then it happened. She saw the recognition in his eyes. "Your physical was Monday," he said. He studied her face so acutely she squirmed from the scrutiny. He accused, "You said everything was okay but you lied, didn't you?"

Offended that he thought she'd outright lie to him, she leaned toward him in rebuttal, "I did not lie and I didn't say it went okay. I said 'it went'."

Her answer fueled his temper, "What did the doctor say and don't leave anything out, you hearin' me loud and clear?"

Kinda hard not to, she nearly replied while staring at his hands. His fists resembled rocks, his handsome face contorted into a scowl guaranteed to terrify small children and put any decent adult on edge. Ennis wasn't just mad, he was furious with her. She hadn't calculated this heated a reaction from him. Sure, she figured he'd be upset – just not murderously upset.

Savannah could barely meet his vision. Trying to hide the news from Ennis festered into such an explosive confrontation, she stumbled for a way to fix it and she finally realized she couldn't...

"Savannah," he prompted. His hands now opened and aimed straight for her shoulders. He meant to follow through on his promise.

Her wide eyes focused on the strong hands headed for her and she blurted, "He found a lump in my left breast."

Instant regret panged hard and heavy in her heart. He'd badgered her into spilling the carefully guarded secret but at least she prevented him from shaking her to bits. His hands not only retreated from her shoulders, they basically dropped dead in the seat.

Exasperation quickly replaced her guilt, "There. Now you know." She rolled the window down, tossed the half eaten Twinkie in the nearby garbage bin and sighed. The difficulty of meeting Ennis's gaze rated up there with walking on the moon. She'd need *a lot* of help getting there before it happened.

The cruiser fell quiet with the exception of the chatter from the police radio and passing traffic on the street ahead of them. Ennis's audible breathing ebbed to nothing with her declaration. She remembered the feeling of not breathing for what seemed minutes.

Upon hearing the doctor's discovery, she swore her whole body shut down. The same feelings flooded back as, from the corner of her vision, she watched her husband's features run a plethora of emotions.

A touch on her shoulder brought a resurgence of tears. Ennis's warm hand curled behind her neck, his gentle urging turned her to face him. "Sugar, we'll get through this together, no matter what the diagnosis is."

She allowed only a couple of tears to fall. "I didn't tell you because I didn't want to burden you with it," her strangled voice managed. "It's not right."

His hand followed the line of her neck to her shoulder, "What's not right is keeping me in the dark. Promise me you'll stop doing that."

She looked away only for Ennis to frame her face with his hands. Despite the cold, his fingers were warm and comforting as he spoke, "Savannah, promise me."

"Ennis, it's not in my nature to share my problems. It's more or less been up to me to fix them. This marriage thing is new to me. Having a man *care* this much is new to me. It'll take time to change…"

"While you're taking that time, remember this," he lectured. "I'm your husband and I want to know when something's wrong. I don't care if it's a hangnail or a health problem. I don't care if you hide it from your daddy or from Seth or Georgia but by God, don't you dare hide it from me. Do you understand?"

Savannah nodded in his hold. His hand clasped hers, "I assume there'll be a biopsy. When is it so I can schedule time off?"

She swallowed hard. With his temper running so hot, she debated telling him the truth. She mulled it over only for the same guilt to plague her stomach again. Lying to Ennis just wasn't in her. "It was Tuesday," she mumbled under her breath. She dreaded his impending tirade. When Ennis truly unleashed his temper, most people cowered. After witnessing his rage during an earlier investigation, she realized pushing Ennis Rutherford to the brink was foolish for anyone. At the current time, she seriously considered exiting the car and running for cover.

The muscles in his jaw tightened as did the grasp on her hand. She attempted to ease his rising fury, "Ennis, I thought I was doing the right thing. I realize I was horribly wrong so please calm down." The explanation heaved more fuel on his blazing mood and she emphasized a final, "Please calm down."

The words ground through clenched teeth, "You went through a breast biopsy by yourself when you knew I'd want to be with you."

She covered his hand with hers in another effort to diffuse his anger, "Ennis, I'm so sorry. I should have included you. I know that now and regret that I didn't."

He uttered an expletive so harsh her mouth fell open. Leaning toward her again, he pinned her with a furious scowl, "I am *not* your daddy. I won't hit you, berate you or say you deserve this."

Savannah's vision sank to her lap. In their time together, Ennis witnessed every one of those moods and heard those very words from R.J.. Her husband held his tongue at her insistence and his resentment toward R.J. finally flared. She stated the obvious, "We wouldn't be married if I thought that."

And, of course, he wasn't convinced, "In the back of your mind you must wonder if all men are like him. I'm not. I am capable of supporting you. I can see you through this if you'll trust me."

"I do trust you. I wanted to save you the worry."

"I want to worry," the ice melted from his tone, "and I want to be there for you."

Savannah's heart squeezed in her chest. Shielding Ennis hurt him more than she ever imagined. She touched his cheek, "Then we'll see it through together, whatever the outcome."

He nodded in agreement, "Together, whatever the outcome. Does the doctor know how big the lump is?"

"He said it looks small."

"When are the results coming in?" His dark eyes narrowed, "Or did I miss that too?"

A momentary peeved frown framed her pursed lips, "No. It was supposed to be today but the doctor hasn't called. I don't guess he's going to until after Christmas." Watching last minute shoppers ease from the parking lot onto the busy street, she asked, "Reckon God has one more miracle in His pocket this year?"

Ennis didn't flinch at the reference to his shooting earlier in the year. She never believed in miracles until then. God gave them a second chance to share their lives and she prayed He allowed them many more years together. For the last few days, she spent her idle time praying. She stayed awake at night to ask God for strength and guidance. Too bad He didn't forewarn her on Monday to include Ennis. Then that night's little Waterloo would have been avoided.

The corners of Ennis's mouth lifted, "He pulled one out for me and I'll bet He's got one with your name on it."

4

Ennis either refused to speak or was too angry to. His hands gripped the steering wheel, his jaw tightened until she saw the muscles repeatedly clench.

Resigning herself to sit back for a night of silence, her mind wandered back to the biopsy. Dr. Wyatt appreciated her level of "concern" – which translated to "fear" in her books and that was more than she could say about most doctors. Maybe it was her white knuckled grasp on the exam table or her wide-eyed visual pursuit of the javelin size needle. Whatever the case, he sensed her panic and inquired if she wanted her husband with her for the procedure.

No, she wanted to say, *I'm not all that excited about my husband seeing how sissified I am when it comes to needles.* For a time she considered asking Georgia to accompany her but later decided against it. Until the results returned, no one needed to know about the biopsy.

Now she glanced at Ennis. So much for the best laid plans…

The car's speed remained reasonable in contrast to his sour expression and death grip on the cruiser's wheel. *Oh, yes, a silent night indeed*, she thought, the irony not lost on her.

She spent the whole week fending off "what if" questions. What if the tumor was malignant? What if she had surgery – then what? What if it spread too far that surgery merely delayed the inevitable? What if she died without a will? Before marrying Ennis, she met the finality of death with a shrug. After the marriage, the thought of dying terrified her. Savannah loved him so much her heart literally ached and the possibility of leaving him generated an unbearable depression.

Trying to relieve the severity of her black mood, she'd made the appointment with Desmond. The morbid exercise of distributing her possessions among people she loved was necessary in case history repeated itself.

Besides leaving Ennis and her siblings specific items, she wanted Lindsey to have certain things of Charlene's. Without having her own daughter, Savannah wanted her niece to inherit a few important heirlooms. Reading from a list she'd assembled in private, she'd spent two hours with the estate lawyer describing in detail how her will should read. She leveled a stern warning before leaving his office, "Call my cell number, not the house. I'll tell Ennis in my own time."

And, as usual, her good intentions backfired big time. At least, she reflected darkly, Ennis wasn't brooding anymore – or backing her against the car door demanding answers. No, he chose to sit behind the wheel and ignore her.

Ennis stopped the car at a red light. He fixated on the steady burning red bulb. Whether he voiced them or not, she sensed him dwelling on questions but mostly stewing over her secretiveness. If he tried to give her a guilt trip, it was too late. She'd already signed up for the one-way ticket.

Savannah peered out the passenger's window to see a young boy bundled up from head to toe like a mini Michelin Man. He held his mother's hand as he stood, eyes wide in awe at the cruiser. When he waved, Savannah waved back. At least *someone* wasn't pissed at her.

She checked her watch. Soon, Seth's kids would pile up in bed, anxiously awaiting Santa's arrival. The year before, Seth resorted to bribing Lindsey with a few extra cookies if she'd just go to bed before nine o'clock. Savannah smirked at her brother's unusual manner of parenting. Seth's wife Leah adopted another approach, "Go to bed this instant or I'll tell Santa you don't want any toys."

This year Lindsey and Dylan carefully composed their letters to Mr. Claus a few days prior to Thanksgiving – to beat the rush Lindsey said. Leah allowed Savannah a glance at each note but the detective's inability to translate Dylan's writing resulted in a comedy of errors. She misinterpreted the entire thing, forcing Leah to decode her young son's wishes. For all the scribbling in green crayon, it simply read "John Deere" so Savannah capitalized and bought him more farm equipment to go with Santa's gifts.

Lindsey, on the other hand, asked for fish. For the past several months, her interests veered from Barbie and a strange obsession with gerbils to raising goldfish. Occasionally adding fish one or two at a time, her room began to resemble the city aquarium. Some held betas while the vast majority housed bubble eye goldfish. According to her letter – which Leah let Savannah sneak a peek at – Lindsey wanted exactly seven more fish, one to represent each of the Seven Dwarfs. The youngster took raising her aquatic friends as seriously as a mother tending her children so while Georgia maintained every girl wanted a baby doll and bought Lindsey one, Savannah headed out to Finn's Fish Emporium and bought a ten gallon aquarium with gravel, a filter and all the trimmings. Then she tossed in a variety of ornaments for the tank and snapped up some books on freshwater fish in case her niece decided to broaden her horizons from goldfish someday.

"You've been awful tired lately," Ennis mentioned offhandedly.

"Ennis, it's Christmas. It goes with the job this time of year. Long shifts and dealing with difficult people who get more difficult when the holidays come 'round."

He finally glanced at her, "So you don't think it's related to your…" He paused a moment, "your breast thing?"

"My breast thing has nothing to do with it." She attempted to reason with him, "Think about it. Aren't you tired after these past few weeks?"

"Yeah, but I don't have breast issues either."

She chuckled, hoping to lighten the mood, "I hope not or I didn't marry who I thought I was marrying."

"Sixteen twelve," the radio called. "Are you back in service?"

With a glance, she referred to Ennis who shrugged, "One or two more calls won't hurt, I guess."

Savannah reached for the mike, "Affirmative. Sixteen twelve is Code Seven."

The dispatcher relayed the call of a food fight at a nearby supermarket. Savannah hit the lights and siren, "What's Christmas without a food fight?"

"A merrier one," Ennis replied.

As they sped away, she glanced in the side view mirror to see the boy pointing toward the car. At that age, police cars enchanted boys more than she ever imagined. When she took Dylan for a spin in one, it thrilled him so much Seth called her later and pleaded for her never to show him one again, "He won't shut up about being a cop."

In contrast, Lindsey's enthusiasm swung to the negative side. She disapproved of Savannah's career choice and with age came bigger, more expressive words to state her opinion. It was too dangerous, she lectured. And, "You'll get shot like Uncle Ennis." Her niece's arguments intensified tenfold after Ennis was shot earlier in the year. Savannah understood her fears and tried unsuccessfully to allay Lindsey's concern. The girl had none of it. On her last visit, Lindsey hugged her neck and whispered to her, "Don't die, okay?" The words haunted her a different way now. Her little niece worried about bad guys and bullets. Little did she know that a lump in Savannah's breast might be her downfall...

The car came to an abrupt halt like a horse pulled up short by the reigns and, like a horse, the cruiser voiced its disapproval. Luckily Savannah braced her hand on the dash in time to avoid her forehead colliding with it. "Ennis, stop driving like an idiot."

To that, he punched the accelerator, sending her back against the seat. She buckled up and slanted him a baleful frown. Once clear of the intersection, he answered, "Sorry 'bout that. That Honda jumped in front of me."

Ennis, bless his sweet heart, loved speed. The streets and highways were his raceway, along with millions of other Atlanta residents dodging, weaving and blasting their way to their destinations. For a

Texas boy accustomed to dirt roads and miles of nothing, he navigated the big city better than a native Georgian.

Such times required seat belts and called for a strong grip on the door handle while the other hand braced against the dash in case of sudden stops. She adopted this technique with her first partner, Riley Murphy, when he introduced her to the NASCAR-style pursuit.

Had Savannah foreseen the night's events, she'd have brought her Dramamine. Ennis's driving left her stomach reeling more times than she cared to count. Thankfully, after he learned of her problem, he eased off the accelerator somewhat – until now, of course, when her stomach teetered on the verge of sickness. The nausea taunted her, letting her know eating half a Twinkie wasn't her most stellar decision.

Snowflakes began floating from the sky only to splatter on the windshield like delicate white bugs as Ennis raced to the next call. Savannah's stomach bounced into her throat when the cruiser scraped bottom exiting an intersection. The rebound sent her a few inches off the seat. "Ennis…"

The car sped into another intersection, causing already harried Christmas Eve shoppers to screech to a halt midway through. Ennis wheeled around the corner, leaving a few unhappy travelers pounding their horns in response to his driving. In her calmest voice, Savannah mentioned, "Ennis, they're having a food fight in the store. No one's drawing their six shooters at high noon."

Ennis didn't respond so she shrugged, "Okay, so maybe they can beat each other to death with a turkey leg or a broom." She glanced over and saw his mask of seriousness break into a genuine smile. That was better, she thought. She wanted his mind off her doctor's visit and onto other subjects because if Ennis's mood fell, hers would plummet.

Savannah cut the siren upon approaching Kroger's. They exited the cruiser to see people gathered on the parking lot. They angled for a peek in the store as the yelling spilled from inside. She shooed them, telling them to go home, "Unless you're a witness, leave. And I can tell you now, all witnesses will go to the station to give their statements. That could take a few hours."

People turned and scattered, the parking lot lights casting long shadows after them. Just as she figured, no one wanted to spend Christmas at a police station, even to give a summation of what transpired between two unbalanced shoppers inside Kroger's. And though it appeared riotous to some that two people fought over groceries, Savannah knew how quickly situations escalated. Emotionally charged people went from heaving fruits and vegetables to ramming heads into walls in a matter of seconds and if one of the combatants grabbed a knife from the utensil aisle, all bets were off…

Another patrol unit arrived and parked beside their car. Two younger cops ranging in age from rookie to veteran stepped out and drew their weapons as Savannah and Ennis had. The older of the two approached her. He raised his voice to be heard over the heated shouting inside, "Dispatch said the caller reported only two people going at it. Sounds like half a dozen of 'em."

"I think one's the manager," she replied. "From what I can see, they're still in the produce department."

Nearing the automatic doors, they heard the shouting inside heighten to threats of bodily harm. "I'll hit you with it, I swear I will!" a male voice warned.

"You do and I'll clock you with this merlot," a woman responded with a shred less volume.

Savannah chanced another peek inside. The man held a string mop like a sword while the female wielded a bottle in one hand in anticipation of whopping her opponent.

Ennis glanced over her shoulder, "At least they don't have knives yet."

"No," she said, "but look out for the merlot. She sounded serious."

"He didn't exactly leave the impression he'd back down either." He addressed the two cops behind him, "You guys ready for this circus?"

They nodded though the younger cop showed the enthusiasm of having a tooth pulled without Novocain. Being a cop sounded exciting until a person hit the street. Then they discovered the reason for bulletproof vests. Savannah appraised the young cop to judge his fear factor. God help them all if anyone actually brandished a gun inside the store. At the angle he held his firearm, she'd get first dibs on a bullet then Ennis followed close behind. "Just back us up," she said. "Put your weapon away."

The rookie gave her a wide-eyed nod and followed her instructions. The group stepped forward, triggering the automatic doors. The sound of them sliding open didn't register with the couple squaring off at the lettuce. The manager, however, seemed completely relieved to see the police. "Oh, thank God," he sighed and waved them closer until seeing their weapons drawn. He instinctively raised his hands and backed away.

The four cops spread out, each ordering the arguing patrons to cease and desist. Savannah and Ennis ventured closer until standing several feet from the feuding pair. "Drop your weapons now," she ordered in a voice commanding compliance. Earlier, Hank ignored her which not only pissed her off but wounded her ego somewhat. This time *everyone* would listen and obey.

The mop struck the floor with a rapport that echoed through the store. The woman lowered the bottle of wine to the floor in a slow, fluid motion. She raised her hands as did the man after surrendering his mop.

When he turned toward Savannah, a wave of laughter threatened to burst from her. The willowy twenty-something white male clearly sensed her battle and frowned, "Don't laugh, 'kay? This bitch is certifiable."

Savannah swallowed her amusement in favor of her own frown, "Well, you don't look too stable either, Gallagher." The reference to the fruit throwing comedian wasn't lost on either participant, considering his opponent's face and clothes sported more tomatoes than a chef salad.

Offended by the detective's comment, the man's mouth slung open which prompted a spontaneous grin from her. His face and hair were covered in a mixture of flour, sugar, and what looked suspiciously like maple syrup. His clothes wore signs of a baker gone awry with a zigzag pattern of syrup crisscrossing his white dress shirt and gray slacks. "What started this fracas in the first place?" Savannah asked, holstering her gun. For safety's sake, she checked their rookie friend in case he got edgy enough to pull his gun. He hadn't.

Returning to the situation at hand, Savannah watched the

woman, her face still slick with tomato juice and pulp, wipe a palm down each cheek then flicked the tiny seeds from her fingers. She drew a deep, quivering breath in an attempt to calm herself before speaking. "I needed a ham for Christmas dinner. I was looking them over," she pointed to a bin freezer twenty yards to their left, "when this maniac starts screaming about dead animals."

"No," he purposefully emphasized, "I told her we shouldn't kill animals just for our holiday gluttony. Do you know how many hogs are slaughtered, how many chickens are killed just to —"

Savannah raised a hand as a "stop" sign, "Tell me how it escalated to *this*." She waved her hand across the chaos before them. Remains of tomatoes mixed with the flour, sugar and syrup created a hodgepodge, multicolored muddle of food. Splatters from the fight freckled the heads of lettuce beside them, and overspray of sugar and flour coated produce in the adjacent bins. People lost their friggin' decency during Christmas, she lamented silently. "Jesus – the Reason for the Season" – a lot of people believed it but few observed it.

The woman dug hunks of sloppy pulp from her hair, "When I didn't concede he was right, he started heaving tomatoes at me. I *had* to defend myself so I used my cake ingredients to fend him off."

Savannah looked to Ennis who, instead of teetering toward laughter, appeared ready to explode. The night wore thin on him as well, especially with her breaking the news of her doctor's visit. His dark mood warned anyone close by to tread carefully around him.

Savannah sighed, "All this over ham?"

The man crossed his arms, "You're not going to arrest me, are you? Come on, it's Christmas, for God's sake."

The mere sound of the words widened his opponent's eyes as though the thought never occurred to her, "B – but I was defending myself. You can't arrest *me*."

Savannah waved off the pleading pair, "If the store manager wants to file charges, you're sunk. If not, you can go home but only after you both clean this mess. Frankly I'm sick of people acting stupid tonight."

The store manager declined to file charges if the arguing patrons agreed to clean the mess. Savannah contributed their eager agreement to Ennis's unpleasant scowl he'd adopted during the call to the supermarket. When his mood headed downhill, blind obedience benefited all who encountered it. The costumers cowered from the scorching look and unyielding set of his jaw.

As a thank-you, the manager handed Ennis, Savannah and the two uniform officers a roast beef sandwich from the store's deli. Both detectives thanked him even though they already had plans that evening. Whenever their shift ended, they were headed to Georgia's for Christmas Eve dinner. No way would Savannah sabotage the upcoming meal. She looked forward to it – even pined for it – for months now, especially the peach pie. Georgia made heavenly peach pies. So heavenly that Savannah filched a whole one for herself, forcing her sister to make two, one for Savannah and the other for the general population's consumption. This year she considered her peach pie a reward for tolerating the public's madness and fate's backhand.

She and Ennis trudged back to the patrol car. Weariness of the day set in hard and when Savannah checked her cell phone to find no messages, she shrugged, resigned. They'd make the best of Christmas and try not to obsess. Between the family activities and seeing Lindsey and Dylan and their Christmas from Santa, there would be plenty to keep her mind busy if she let it.

Light snow still drifted down from the sky and the wind temporarily diminished. Savannah knew her niece and nephew sang the praises of Christmas snow. Plans for building snowmen the next day were being discussed – along with Seth's no-nonsense advice, "There's not enough to roll into a golf ball, much less a snowman." Savannah could hear Leah, the optimist of the two, "Wait till morning and I'll bet there's enough to play in."

At times her brother's charm rivaled Scrooge. She wasn't sure if the army yanked the dreamer out of him but he changed after returning home. It was another reason she intended to keep her secret as long as possible. Without intending to, Seth would say something to set her off or depress her.

Ennis looked into the gray sky, "How much snow is forecast?"

She felt his hand settle at the small of her back as they walked back to the cruiser. He angled toward the driver's side, leaving her to ride shotgun again. She answered, "A couple of inches or six to eight, depending on who you believe."

"First one sounds better. These people drive deranged no matter the weather."

An impulsive smile surfaced at his description. He missed the irony of his remark. "It reminds me of your driving," she joked.

To her surprise, he took offense, "What's that supposed to mean? Does my driving piss you off that bad?"

Ever since they partnered up, she'd teased him about his driving. It was a running joke between the two. There *were* a few times he literally made her sick but she held her complaints to a minimum if possible. He almost always took the banter in stride – until tonight.

Savannah leaned against the cruiser, "Ennis, do we need to talk?" They stared at each other for several seconds and she saw a rising anger building in him. She assumed it was directed at her for keeping secrets and hiring lawyers.

Their visual showdown ended when Ennis folded his arms on the roof, "We've been married less than six months."

Savannah broke eye contact. For several days she'd agonized over the same fact. Life hadn't been easy for them since they began working together. Between Ennis's shooting and now the possibility of her having cancer, Savannah wondered if their lives would ever settle down. "I've thought about that too." She felt grateful fate was the cause of his resentment instead of her.

He pounded his fist against the metal roof, "Damn it, we can't catch a break."

His fist left a dent in the roof, a fact he ignored and also appeared he entertained bashing it again. Savannah waited, watched him agonize over thoughts he couldn't put into words. Emotionally he traveled the same road she'd traversed for days. Once the shellshock subsided, the denial took its place then the inevitable questions trickled in. It started slow then after digesting the news, a flood of whys and what ifs swamped a person. The range of emotion staggered her but the worst turned out to be the anger. It crept in at odd times – at work, watching TV or simply reading a book. She wanted to hit something all the time but she leveled her rage on people who smiled. How could they be happy when her life could be falling completely apart? "Ennis," she said in a gentle tone, "I don't know if it's malignant or not. Until Dr. Wyatt calls, it's a fifty-fifty split. I'm trying to stay positive about it. You should too." She said it with a conviction she lacked. Honestly, she was terrified to find out because of her family history. Dr. Wyatt emphasized that family history didn't automatically mean malignancy, but in her heart, Savannah knew. So far no one in the family with breast issues emerged unscathed by the disease.

Ennis nodded, "I'm just…" his voice trailed to silence.

"Overwhelmed and scared," she offered.

"Yeah, that's it." His finger circled the dent he left, "You mind if I call Ma and tell her? The more prayers, the better."

Savannah debated the request. If he called his mother, she'd call Dane who, in turn, would alert Georgia who'd tell Seth then he'd blab to his wife Leah who was a nurse. The vast and speedy network of communication staggered her. One couldn't swear a member to secrecy because none of them grasped the word's meaning. She didn't need the hassle of lectures or, worse, pep talks at a time she just wanted to forget.

"Can you wait a while? I don't want Georgia finding out through the back channels. I'll never hear the end of it." Movement behind Ennis caught her eye and she tilted to the side. A cocker spaniel, its fur matted and muddy, wandered close to the cruiser. "Ennis, look behind you."

He swiveled on his heel to see the cocker tuck its tail and duck its head. It shied away from making eye contact with either detective. Savannah retrieved her sandwich from the dash then eased around the back of the car. The dog cowered at the sudden movement. The large brown eyes shifted between her and Ennis, debating over whether to chance an encounter with the strangers. *The poor thing looks ragged, hungry and exhausted.* Savannah thought. *Kinda like me.*

She bent to one knee, her voice gentle as she called the cocker. Sad, dark eyes glanced up at her, eyes weary of presenting a cautious but brave front. Eyes that also looked downright lonely, Savannah noticed. She kept calling the dog while unwrapping the sandwich. She pinched off a bite of roast beef, "C'mere, girl. Here's some Christmas supper for you."

The cocker's nose twitched, its eyes suddenly brightened as the aroma of roast beef wafted toward her. Savannah held out her hand, the food in her palm. The puppy baby-stepped closer.

"You just made her pee," Ennis chuckled.

As the shaggy little creature ventured nearer, a trail of pee followed in its wake. Savannah replied, "If I looked like her and someone offered me a meal, I'd probably pee from excitement too."

He started to bend down, "Hey, she's got a collar."

His partner shook her head, stopping him, "Not yet. Let her eat a little first, get our trust then we'll check the collar."

The grateful cocker nibbled at the offering then Savannah felt the gentle scraping of teeth on her fingers as the puppy's appetite finally kicked in. Offering a larger portion of meat, Savannah dared to pet the dog, her fingers stroking the damp, knotted fur. The pup risked stepping closer while soaking up the sweet talk and gentle petting.

A smile curved Savannah's mouth, her voice remained low and soft, "Grab a blanket from the trunk. I think we're finally bonding."

Ennis basically tiptoed to the trunk. A minute later, he handed a small blanket off to his wife, careful not to spook the puppy.

Savannah sat the sandwich on the ground. The cocker converged on the sizeable meal, giving the female detective a chance to wrap the blanket around her. The dog resisted somewhat when Savannah lifted her into her arms. It made a point of whimpering its disappointment of leaving the meal behind.

Drawing her closer, Savannah shushed her, "It's okay. Here's your food." When she picked up the sandwich, the puppy stretched for the meat until voraciously consuming every morsel. It reminded Savannah of how she pined for Georgia's peach pie. One whiff and she warned the masses to clear the area while she swooped in to devour the dessert.

"I'll go get some water from the store," Ennis said. "Fast as it's eating, that dog's either gonna dehydrate or spew like a volcano."

"The address says 3805. Turn here and it'll shortcut into the thirty-eight hundred block."

Ennis nodded at her instructions. As long as he'd lived in Atlanta, there were still die-does and shortcuts he'd yet to discover. When in uniform, Savannah traversed all the city zones as, she assumed, most rookies and uniform officers do. In her travels, she noted obvious abbreviated routes for faster response time.

The neighborhood was quiet for Christmas Eve. Some driveways stood empty while others teemed with cars. She could imagine families conversing and laughing and rooms filled with aromas of ham and spice – and the sound of wrapping being ripped from gifts.

The patrol car eased down the street and they both counted off addresses until 3805 came into view. "Looks quiet." She glanced at her watch, "Wonder if they're gone."

Ennis pulled next to the curb. He killed the engine and the two observed the house for activity. "Nice house," he noticed.

The two story homes here were about her age and were built in the old manor style where large families lived without feeling cramped for space. 3805 looked smaller than its neighbors with a well kept lawn and quaint, modest appearance. It, like the puppy in Savannah's arms, was probably the runt of the bunch but also probably the best. "Nice part of town," she added. "Not many calls to this area when I patrolled here."

Ennis pointed to the upper story where a light blinked on, "Someone's home."

During the ride, the small cocker fell asleep in Savannah's arms. The sight warmed her heart. Somehow dogs responded to her more than kids. Besides speculating on what that actually meant, she wondered if the dog sensed their desire to help.

She gingerly lifted the sleeping bundle into her arms while Ennis got out, opened the door for her. She readjusted the blanket to protect the puppy from the bitter wind and snow. "Poor little thing," Savannah whispered. "No telling how long she's been on her own."

The two detectives padded their way up the semi-circle drive to the porch. Ennis thumbed the doorbell once. What once appeared empty, the house suddenly came alive in light, from a top story window to the bottom entry. To cap off the illumination, the porch light winked on just before Savannah heard a deadbolt slide back and a lock snap open.

Light flooded the long veranda-type porch. The door swung open with a groan to reveal a young woman standing in a fluffy, sky blue robe. She stood about Savannah's height and her heavy-lidded blank stare indicated a mother who'd had just about enough of Christmas for one year. Even when she blinked, it was with great effort.

The two women exchanged a "where have I seen you before" look before the bleary-eyed woman passed an indifferent, nearly glazed stare over the two, "Can I help you?"

"Ma'am," Ennis began, "we're with the police..." His sentence trailed off into oblivion since the woman appeared to be two steps away from unconscious and slipping fast.

Savannah watched the woman's vision drift down until settling on the sleeping bundle in her visitor's arms. Then she suddenly jolted awake, startling not only the detectives but the puppy as well. "Oh my God, you found her!" Tears sprung from her once sleepy eyes while she reached for the puppy, "You two are lifesavers. My kids wouldn't ask Santa for anything except Paris. They were so depressed because she was gone but you found her! Thank you!"

"Paris?" Savannah inquired, her brain gradually cranking out the answer to the mystery.

"The mall!" the woman cried. "You two were the officers at the mall tonight. *That's* where I've seen you!"

"You're Sarah's mother, right?" Though it was hard to tell with the tangled bird's nest atop the woman's head. A few hours earlier, she'd looked the epitome of Christmas elegance with her red sweater, green pants and her silky dark hair pulled into a ponytail.

Wide awake and swiping tears of joy, the woman nodded. Savannah smiled at her, "You have a Merry Christmas, ma'am. And tell Sarah Merry Christmas for us."

"I will," she lifted the wriggling pup closer as if to ensure she was really there, "It's a Christmas miracle and you two are angels. Wait till I tell Sarah."

Savannah thought about that. The title of angel made her blush considering she'd rarely – if ever – been described as such on the job. Little Sarah specifically asked Santa to return the puppy. So... "On second thought, let Santa take the credit. I don't think he'll mind."

5

Every woman feared breast cancer whether it ran in the family or not. Family history increased hers and Georgia's chances. Difference was Georgia got regular mammograms and Savannah didn't. Her sister cultivated her knack for haranguing over the years. Georgia could nag a monk to suicide, their father once said. She'd heard as much about early detection from Georgia as she had about getting shot and dying from Lindsey. Savannah swore her sister tutored their niece in the fine art of badgering. The two never grasped the fact that nagging only made things worse. Getting a mammogram rated in the realm of having a root canal. She wasn't about to do it unless absolutely necessary. Her last one left her sore for a week when Mistress Torment squashed her boobs to the thickness of a postage stamp. She vowed never again unless Mistress brought a well fortified army with her. Now a simple physical turned into a veritable nightmare, all because it was too inconvenient and painful. She felt fine so why bother? When the doctor discovered the lump, she finally realized why...

She retreated inward with the news as she always had. To burden others with her problems seemed wrong, therefore if keeping silent kept her conscience clear, she did it. Ennis would never understand that part of her. She never expected him to.

A warm hand covered hers, squeezed it gently, "You okay?"

His tender hold and soft voice pulled her from her thoughts. Turning to him, she smiled and gave a slight nod.

"You're not thinking negatively about this biopsy, are you?" he asked.

"Nope." *Liar...* She'd forced her answer and hoped he hadn't noticed. In her heart, she realized he did.

Savannah pulled her cell phone from her belt, opened it and checked for messages. None. A wave of disappointment engulfed her. Apparently, the doctor wasn't calling until after the holiday. He promised the results by week's end so where the hell were they? What was worse, she wondered. Waiting and not hearing or not waiting and getting the call so she could plod through Christmas with a fake smile? At least this way she could honestly claim ignorance to the questions her family would ask. Wow, she thought. What a consolation...

She clipped the phone back to her belt with a sigh. Ennis tightened his hold, "No news yet?"

"Nothing. Guess it'll be next week."

"We'll get through this together, sugar. I'm with you every step of the way."

She nodded, not trusting herself to speak without tears. If she managed to successfully plod through Christmas without the world knowing her plight, she'd give herself a damn gold star. The last thing she needed or wanted were the "looks" people gave when they heard such news. Her mother's side handed out pity like candy on Halloween and very few offered genuine support. Most looked upon the stricken with anticipation of disaster.   "One foot in the grave" was a Culberson trait. R.J. couldn't stand it and neither could she. Savannah remembered a Culberson family picnic when R.J. endured the death talk (and who was afflicted with what maladies) for a solid hour and a half. He nursed his scotch until growing completely fed up with it all. He leaned toward Charlene and basically shouted, "If you ever start talkin' that way, you'll turn our kids into psychotics like the rest of your family." All talk ceased at that point while all eyes centered on Charlene. Savannah expected her mother to bow out of the picnic immediately, apologizing as she went. Charlene laughed instead, telling R.J. he was right.

She wished her mother was still alive. Every Christmas she missed her more. Time didn't heal all wounds. Whoever said it never lost someone dear to them. Time only deepened the void left by the person's passing. It left a hollowness no one could fill.

The dispatcher broadcast an accident in close proximity to their location, "All available units respond." Savannah radioed they were on the way.

Just as she switched on the lights and siren, her cell phone rang with the familiar Elvis tune "A Little Less Conversation". She jerked the phone from her belt, hoping it was Dr. Wyatt. It wasn't.

"I was calling to see if your shift was over but judging by the siren, it's obviously not," Georgia said.

"It's the longest one of my career. I'll let you know when we're done, okay?"

"No hurry. I'm still baking the sweet potato pies for tomorrow.

Just drop in when you can."

Savannah ended the conversation as Ennis zigzagged through traffic. She held the complaints to a minimum. If anyone was seriously injured, they needed help fast.

Closer to the accident scene, traffic began slowing to a stop. The road resembled a runway with two lanes of brake lights illuminating the way. The traffic jam forced Ennis to the emergency lane for a clear route. Dozens of cars lined one behind the other, their impatient drivers remained in the cozy confines of their vehicles. A few used their horns to voice their displeasure of the delay. Savannah leashed her anger. In years past, people rushed to help at accidents instead of ignoring the fact someone might be dying in front of them. Now they refused to lift a finger except their middle one.

Their headlight beams sliced through the blackness of night, revealing the horrific aftermath of two vehicles colliding. A pickup crashed into an eighties model Buick Skylark, leaving the latter basically a crumpled heap. Steam and smoke rose from the two vehicles as the cruiser neared the scene. Ennis parked several yards from the accident.

Savannah's heart sank with the likelihood no one in the car probably survived. "Oh my God," was all she brought herself to say.

"Do you think anyone's alive?" Ennis whispered back.

Still stunned by the devastation, she shook her head, "I don't know." She *did* know the clock was ticking on survivors if there were any. She tried to prepare herself for the worst. Judging from the extent of damage and position of the vehicles, Savannah surmised the pickup was traveling at a high rate of speed and ran into the Skylark on the intersecting road.

Savannah radioed their arrival and requested more units for traffic control and, "Get ambulances and F.D. out here now." She exited the car, flashlight in hand, "You take the pickup and I'll check the car." She tossed a baleful glare over her shoulder, "Since these fine citizens couldn't be bothered to help."

A nearby car blasted its horn as if complaining about the wait. She turned, her anger finally breaking free, "Touch that horn again and I'll shove it in a place only your proctologist can reach it."

Except for a few groans from the cars, an eerie silence fell over the scene. A thin veil of acrid smoke hung between the two as Savannah swept the narrow beam across the cars. Light reflected off crumpled chrome and bits of glass sparkled like diamonds as the beam passed across.

Savannah called out, identifying herself, hoping to hear a response from the Buick as she approached. Fluids from the cars dripped onto the asphalt, one of them smelling like gasoline. In a quick pass of the flashlight, Savannah noticed the rainbow sheen of oil and gas seeping into a large, expanding pool around the cars. Closer examination revealed a Stop sign trapped and mangled beneath the Skylark. With an impact that severe, she guessed, the post or sign might have sliced into the gas tank. "Ennis, gas is leaking from the car so be careful."

She heard him speaking to the driver of the pickup while she hurried around the driver's side of the car. A woman in her mid-twenties slumped over the steering wheel, her face bloodied with a fresh trail trickling from a gash on her forehead.

Savannah tried to rouse her, "Ma'am, can you hear me?" The

woman remained motionless and Savannah reached inside the broken window to feel for a pulse. She felt a faint drumming against her fingertips. She called the woman again, this time in a louder voice.

The woman's pale green eyes slowly blinked, "My son," was the faint whisper. "Is my son okay?"

Savannah swung the flashlight to the passenger seat but found no child. She moved to the back to see a child's car seat securely buckled in. Inside the seat was a small child in a blue jumper and matching jacket. He wasn't moving. "Your son's still in the car seat." Savannah reached through the shattered driver's window to unlock the back door. When she tried opening it, she found it jammed shut like the front door. She braced one foot against the car for leverage as she labored to pop the door open.   Finally it released, allowing her to reach in to feel for the child's pulse. His skin felt warm and showed no signs of outward injury.

Her cool fingers touched the baby's neck and startled the infant awake, his crying filling the interior of the crushed car. A huge wave of relief washed over Savannah, "He seems to be okay. Ma'am, we've got help coming so try not to move."

The woman whispered something else and the detective leaned closer to hear. With great effort the woman repeated, "Is my daughter okay?"

Panic flooded Savannah. There was no child in the car except the baby. She swung the flashlight into the back seat again then the passenger floorboard. What she saw robbed her breath and composure. Coloring books scattered across the floorboard. A Barbie doll lay upside down against the door. She aimed the flashlight at the shattered windshield now collapsed onto the mangled hood in a thousand tiny cubes of glass. *The girl must have been thrown from the car during impact...* "Oh God," Savannah whispered under her breath. She addressed the mother, "I'll be back. Just hang in there."

Savannah frantically passed the flashlight across the side of the road. Pages from coloring books littered the pavement, all drawn in bright, vibrant colors. She passed by a yellow lion then by another drawing, this one a white lamb with a strawberry colored nose.

The breeze blew several loose pages along the road's edge and into the nearby ravine. She pulled her jacket around her to combat the bitter breeze. The snow began to pick up again, the flakes bigger and wetter than before.

Savannah called out but heard nothing but the rattling of the pages blowing further down the road. In a louder voice she tried again while still searching the overgrown ravine for a girl around Lindsey's age.

The flashlight caught a splash of lime green and yellow. Savannah ran toward it. Glancing down at the young girl in the colorful dress, she briefly closed her eyes, forced the rising sickness down.

She peeled off her suit jacket and kneeled beside the girl to cover her from the bitter wind. Blood soaked one side of her long, golden hair and Savannah saw a slashing cut across the girl's scalp. Dozens of small cuts speckled her arms and face. Savannah knew better than to move the girl from the patch of weeds she'd landed in. With the external injuries, there were internal ones too, she'd bet her own life on it.

When she called to the girl, her eyes slowly opened and Savannah summoned her calmest voice, "Hey, sweetheart." She adjusted the jacket over the girl's shoulders, "Maybe this will keep the wind off until help arrives."

"I hurt," the small voice replied.

Savannah's trembling hand carefully brushed a few strands of hair from the girl's face then felt her cheek. The skin, unlike the boy's, felt cool beneath her touch, "I know you do, baby, and help's coming. You'll be alright, just stay awake for the ambulance. Can you do that for me?"

She cringed, "I'll try. Where's Mommy?"

"Mommy's close by and she's gonna get help too. Let me go tell her you're okay and I'll be right back."

She moved slightly beneath the jacket, crying, "I want Mommy and I want my teddy."

The show of emotion twisted Savannah's heart. She couldn't move the girl or take her to her mother. The mere act of lifting her would cause untold damage, "Sweetheart, calm down. I'll find your teddy but try not to cry." Savannah rose to her feet, swinging the flashlight in a frantic search for a teddy bear somewhere in the forest of weeds and grass.

"Savannah!" Ennis shouted from the pickup. She wheeled as he asked, "You find another victim?"

"A girl!" she shouted back.

"There's just the driver in the truck and he's tanked out of his mind. Bastard tried to bolt on me so I cuffed him to the steering wheel."

"Good. Can you tell the girl's mother I found her daughter and she's alive?"

Ennis nodded. She couldn't bear to say more. The girl was alive for now and if paramedics arrived soon she stood a chance of surviving.

Scrapping together her meager knowledge of physics, Savannah finally ran across a white teddy bear wearing a pink dress that read "Hayley".

Hurrying back to the child, she brushed dirt and grass from the bear before handing it to her, "Here's your teddy, sweetheart. Your name is Hayley?"

A pained nod answered her, the girl's bloodied hand gripped the bear's paw and squeezed. The detective touched her cheek. It was still cooler than it should have been, "Mine's Savannah. You're gonna be alright, Hayley. Help's on the way for you and your mommy and brother."

Hayley's eyes drifted closed but she managed a nod. Off in the distance, Savannah spotted the flashing lights of emergency vehicles, "Hayley, they're just about here. Open your eyes for me, sweetheart. Come on, show me those pretty blue eyes."

The lids fluttered then barely opened. Savannah touched her cheek and cringed. The skin felt colder now.

"Savannah!" Ennis yelled. Terror laced her husband's voice and she wheeled to see flames dancing beneath the smaller, older car. In that small amount of time, a trail of gasoline snaked along the road into the ravine. Wind-whipped flames charged along the trail as Ennis ran toward her, "Grab the kid and run. I'm getting the boy out before the whole car goes up."

Panic and adrenaline took over as she scooped Hayley into her arms. Despite the girl's cries, Savannah cradled her while running. "I'm sorry, baby. I'm trying not to hurt you but I have to run."

The fire roared into the ravine as Savannah headed toward the pavement. She watched Ennis unfasten the car seat and bring the baby to the cruiser. Without a word, he raced toward the drunk's pickup. Savannah stopped him, "Leave that bastard for last. He's the reason this whole thing happened. We'll get the mother first!"

Redirecting his efforts back to the car, Ennis warned, "You stay put. She's dead but I'll try to get her out."

"Be careful!" she hollered back. Her heart sank at the news of the mother. Losing one's mother at any age was traumatic enough but at Hayley's age, Savannah couldn't imagine how hard life would be without a mother's guidance.

She glanced down at the girl whose breathing grew quick and shallow. "Stay with me, Hayley. Help's about here."

The flames grew taller and angrier as they licked from beneath the bottom of the car. Savannah heard yelling from the pickup but ignored it. The fire wasn't even close to the driver. She'd let the son of a bitch sweat a little longer before saving him.

Ennis pulled at the Buick's door to no avail. The car rocked back and forth with the effort but the smashed door refused to open. Savannah saw him struggling to pry the door loose. "I'll come help you!" she offered.

Ennis leveled a scathing warning on her, "Stay the hell where you are. I can't get this open anyway. It's stuck."

Flames suddenly exploded from the beneath the car, engulfing it. She watched in horror as frenzied orange and white fire rolled over the car, encasing it in a blazing fury no one could survive.

"Ennis!" she cried. The fire roared like a giant, hungry beast intent on devouring everything in its path. Intense heat backed Savannah up a few steps as she searched for her husband behind the wall of flames.

Nausea rolled and boiled like the fire before her. She prayed Ennis hadn't been caught in the fire. The undulating barrier of heat and flame prevented her from seeing past its furor and the burning ravine blocked her access on one side, leaving only one passage to save Ennis.

She started around the drunk's pickup, ignoring his pleas for help when Ennis emerged from behind the windswept blaze. He met her at the pickup, his hands working feverishly to uncuff the driver while lecturing her, "I told you to stay put now go back to the cruiser. I don't want you near these cars if they blow."

A lecture never sounded so sweet. Just seeing Ennis alive and – from first glance – unscathed nearly sent her to her knees to thank God. Tears welled in her eyes as she nodded and headed back to the cruiser along with him and the driver. Ennis locked the driver's hands behind his back, sat him in the back of the car.

Sweeping tears away with her shoulder, she attempted to keep her voice steady. It failed miserably, "You scared me to death. I thought the fire –"

"I'm okay," he assured between heaving breaths. He leaned on his knees, taking deep breaths to calm down, "Rattled but okay."

Savannah praised God. Stress and emotions tipped the scale for the past several minutes. Horrifying scenes tormented her, scenes that shook a person to the soul. Scenes of losing someone so dear that living without them seemed pointless. If Ennis had been caught in the fire…

The weight in her arms grew heavier as she turned away from the burning vehicles. Savannah shielded Hayley from the gruesome sight unfolding in the Buick.

She cradled the girl, calling her name. The little girl's eyes remained closed, her small body motionless in her arms. "Hayley," she beckoned, "sweetheart, wake up."

Ennis straightened, evidently hearing her distress. He bent closer to the child as Savannah called her name. He pressed his fingertips against Hayley's neck for a pulse.

"The ambulance is here," Savannah lifted the girl closer and felt for breath against her cheek, "Please open your eyes."

The limp form beneath her jacket didn't respond. Tears fell down Savannah's cheeks, "They're finally here to help you."

"Savannah," Ennis spoke softly, his tone affirming what she refused to accept.

"No," she wept, holding the child closer. "She's just sleeping."

"Sugar, she's not breathing, there's no pulse. She's gone." He reached to take Hayley from her embrace.

Savannah wheeled, rejecting his effort, "She's not *gone*." Kneeling, she placed the girl on the pavement and stripped the jacket away.

"What are you doing?" he asked.

"CPR. She's not going to die if I can help it."

He touched her shoulder only for her to twist free of his hand. Tears blinded her eyes and choked her voice, "Ennis, I have to try."

His fingers closed around her arm and tried pulling her to her feet, "Sugar, nothing can be done. Look at her. *Look at her.*"

A tidal wave of emotion broke over. Weeping inconsolably,

Savannah saw the severity of the girl's wounds. With the jacket removed, Hayley's injuries became glaringly evident. One leg bent at an awkward angle and Savannah saw bone protruding halfway up the calf. Hayley's other leg also appeared broken and crushed in places. She looked like a broken rag doll, her once cheerful bright dress now stained and covered in blood.

Savannah brushed the hair from the girl's face, her hand touched her cheek. The skin was colder now. She couldn't bear to think about the broken ribs inside the small body, ribs that punctured lungs or the liver or heart. She knew carrying the child posed a serious threat but she couldn't live with herself if the fire claimed Hayley. Instead, she now shouldered another burden. Trying to save the child from a fiery death – simply moving her, had killed her…

In the gentlest manner possible, Savannah gathered the child's broken body in her arms again, rose to her feet. She held her close as she cried, her overwhelmed mind struggling to make sense to the night's and week's events. Hayley wasn't the first child to pass away in her arms but she was the youngest. At those times, Savannah bit her tongue against cursing God. Children shouldn't die, she wanted to scream at Him. Children should grow up to live happy lives as adults. The fairytale mentality resided in every decent human being, she assumed. Kids were supposed to be immune to danger, protected against such pain.

From behind the traffic jam, an ambulance rolled up ahead of two fire engines. Two paramedics, trauma kits in hand, rushed toward Savannah and the girl. "Who needs medical attention?" one asked.

Savannah swallowed her bitter response. Through narrowed eyes, she assessed their "emergency medical team". They consisted of two kids barely out of high school. Those two kids, in her opinion, valued quick response time as much as they valued socks for Christmas. She'd seen the type before. They probably stopped off for a burger before responding to the accident. And as for the idiotic question "who needs medical attention", they were both about to need it once she leveled them.

One paramedic's vision trailed downward to focus on Savannah, "Detective, you're bleeding. Come with me –"

"*I'm* not bleeding," she seethed with mounting rage. "This little girl is bleeding. If you'd been two minutes earlier..." Her tirade backed the paramedic *and* Ennis off a step. Warm tears rolled down her cheeks only to turn as cold as her voice, "Just two minutes."

The paramedic cut his vision to Ennis. His lifted brow basically inquired if Savannah had come unhinged. Interpreting the insinuation, Ennis volleyed back a twin of his wife's angry scowl.

The paramedic backpedaled, "I'm sorry, Detective. We drove as fast as possible but it's Christmas Eve." He pointed behind him, "The traffic is terrible."

The mention of the holiday brought a wave of tears that she couldn't control, no matter how she tried. She spoke softly as if the child were asleep in her arms, "Her name is Hayley." The words wavered on her unsteady voice, "She's cold. Can you cover her with a blanket?"

The unexpected shift in Savannah's mood put the paramedic in a guarded, uneasy posture. He nodded then offered to take the girl. Savannah brought her closer, placed a kiss on her forehead, whispering, "I'm sorry, baby. I tried to help you." She relinquished custody of the child, carefully placing her in the paramedic's cradled arms.

Savannah realized she still held the little girl's teddy bear, "Wait. She needs her teddy." She felt Ennis's hand on her shoulder as she placed the bear on Hayley's chest, "Make sure he stays with her."

"Yes, ma'am," the paramedic replied and turned toward the ambulance, the child's lifeless limbs swinging with his stride.

Savannah turned away from the image. Her vision swept across her pink pullover. Crimson red blood streaked and pooled so heavily in places, the fabric had a macabre, almost black appearance. The cold sensation on her arms came from the bitter wind blowing across the thick coating of blood. Hayley's blood. She recoiled, "Ennis…"

Ennis lifted her chin until her tear-filled vision met his sympathetic but stern expression, "Don't look at it. I'll get some towels from the trunk and clean you up until we get to the station and you can change clothes. Just don't look at it."

"All that blood and I never felt it. I didn't know, Ennis. I didn't know she was bleeding that bad and I picked her up and ran with her. I killed her."

"No," the word shot out hot and fierce enough it not only surprised Savannah but made the paramedics pause also. Ennis's large hands framed her face, holding her attention strictly on him, "You saved her from burning to death. She was going to die either way."

Ennis was right but her brain refused to accept it. It rejected any justification of her actions.

Her husband's grasp hardened a degree, "Savannah, do you hear me? She was going to die no matter what you did or didn't do. You saved her the pain of burning to death."

The harsh reality of the child's death broke her one unraveling thread of composure. She buried her face in Ennis's chest, her hands fisted in his jacket as she sobbed, "I can't do this anymore. I can't watch kids die. I just can't."

For the first time since Ennis had known her, Savannah collapsed in his arms, crying. The severity of her breakdown scared him to the point he wanted her to retire from the job the instant they returned to the station. He considered the knee-jerk declaration a natural response. Holding a badly injured child that passed away in his arms probably would bring the same announcement stated in the same vehement manner. Visions of Lindsey haunted Savannah, Ennis realized that. Since the girls shared the same approximate age, she saw her niece in her arms instead of little Hayley. The fact Lindsey was at home asleep and awaiting Santa's arrival failed to burrow through the trauma of Hayley's death.

Once he settled Savannah's crying, he and the paramedics cleaned the blood from her arms. The small group gathered in the ravine for the procedure and Ennis draped his suit jacket around her shoulders to warm her and help calm her trembling. He hoped it succeeded at the former because she still shivered like a leaf in a storm.

As the paramedics rinsed the blood off, she watched the dark pink blend of water and blood cascade down her forearms and fingers. The sickening sight reminded Ennis of a Friday the 13th movie, only the reality of death came in actual sights, smells and textures and not on a TV screen where pressing the Stop button ended the horror.

Several minutes later she sat in the patrol car, her vision staring at

– or rather through – the floorboard. Squatting beside the open cruiser door, Ennis heard an occasional sniffle and finally touched her thigh, hoping to break her trance. It didn't.

"I'll take you home," he offered. "I'll call Georgia and tell her what happened. She'll understand."

She blinked then shook her head. Her apparent despair mixed with resignation worried him. Her vacant, almost haunted stare concerned him most. His heart told him she was poised on a dangerous precipice where one more prod might nudge her over the edge. "She can take the food to Seth's and eat with them," he added.

Her voice was lifeless, monotone, "The kids are in bed."

Checkmate, Ennis thought. He searched for another solution, "Do you need to talk to Georgia? She's a good listener –"

"She doesn't need this image in her mind. It's not fair to dump it on her." She sighed, "Let's just go back to the station and get the hell out of there."

Ennis touched her hand, gave it a gentle squeeze, "Okay." His brow sank at her indifferent tone. Everyone reached their limit as a law enforcement officer. Savannah proved herself a tough woman on the job. But dealing with the accident and the possibility of having breast cancer could bring the strongest contender to their knees.

He rounded the front of the cruiser, glanced at her. She refused to look toward the burned-out shell of the Skylark. She averted her gaze to the overgrown field beside the patrol car. The fire burned within a few feet of the cruiser before the fire department gained control of it. Wisps of smoke rose from the charred ravine and mixed with the smell of burned upholstery, metal, rubber and human remains. The sickening combination choked him and he wrapped his arm across his face to block the brunt of it.

He got in and slammed the door in hopes of sealing them away from the smells. The passenger door remained wide open and Savannah showed no signs of closing it. Her blank stare still held strong. He should have shut the door for her, he griped at himself. She wasn't exactly in the mood to care about smells.

Trails of smoke still wafted from the charred Buick. The children's mother had long been removed from the wreckage but Savannah still avoided looking in the general direction.

"Babe," he mentioned softly, "you want me to close your door?"

She reached for the handle and pulled the door shut. Her defeated manner and posture convinced him she might require professional help to cope with the stress of the biopsy and the horrible accident. At some point that night, he would ask Georgia her opinion when Savannah was out of the room. If he mentioned a shrink, his wife would stare at him like he was the village idiot. Only her sister stood a chance of bringing up the taboo subject without risk of bodily harm.

Seconds stretched into long, silent minutes as Ennis drove to the station. Every mile seemed like a lifetime. From the corner of his eye, Ennis gauged Savannah's mood. She ignored Christmas lights and festive decorations adorning the passing homes. He forced himself to watch the road instead of his wife. In their years as partners, they saw human degradation, the scum of humanity and brutality beyond anyone's imagination. They investigated homicides with victims of all ages. The accident tonight triggered a severe, almost catatonic response from a woman he thought he knew completely.

Before setting off to the station, Ennis placed her bloodied suit jacket in the back seat and left his own jacket around her shoulders to not only warm her but help hide her pullover. He was grateful they kept a change of clothes in their lockers. They rarely needed them but tonight he praised their preparedness. The trick would be getting past the desk sergeant without fielding crass jokes concerning their detective's car. If the sergeant listened close enough, his officers told him about the accident and perhaps might save the jokes for later when everyone's nerves had time to mend. Once inside the station, Ennis discovered the sergeant either possessed no class or never listened to his officers.

"Hey, Prince!" Sergeant Roth yelled loud enough to stir surrounding interest, "You need a detective's refresher course if you can't find your own car!"

"Save it," Ennis barked back. "We've had a lousy night."

The distinct sound of restrained laughter brought a mild flare-up from Savannah, "Whenever you guys think you can do this job better, I suggest you put in for a promotion."

Nearby officers uttered a low, rising "ooh" in response. It reminded Ennis of bullies in a schoolyard, picking on the new kid. They turned to the sergeant in anticipation of a comeback. Ennis and Savannah also expected it from the gruff, middle-aged and over-ranked man. Roth's reputation as a smartass preceded him throughout the department and Ennis suspected his promotion came about to transfer him from one station to another – their station unfortunately.

The room fell unusually quiet with only the chatter from their radios. Ennis kept a guarded ear tuned to the potbellied fathead standing behind the desk while guiding Savannah toward the locker room. He'd set Sergeant Roth straight if need be. *Leave my partner alone...*

"It ain't me that's got the beef with you anyhow," Roth yielded to the disappointment of his officers. "Jeffries is the one gunnin' for you both."

Savannah shrugged with a fair amount of weariness, "He can wait in line."

The sergeant's smirk triggered Ennis's temper, "You deaf or something, Roth?" Since the egotistical lamebrain needed a picture drawn, he'd get it vividly illustrated. Ennis leaned across the desk, kept his voice low to prevent her overhearing, "We were first on scene at that accident where the mother and daughter died. Prince tried to save the little girl but the kid died in her arms so do you mind?"

The explanation – and the harsh delivery of the request – appeared to sober the sergeant. He hollered an apology to Savannah who waved it off. By the time Ennis caught up with her, he saw her standing at the locker room door. Stepping inside provided a respite from the rabble of noise and voices of the station, bringing the volume to a negligible hum.

She shrugged out of his jacket then peeled off the bloody pullover which she tossed onto a nearby bench. Standing at the sink in only her bra and slacks, she began scrubbing her arms with soap. Ennis watched her relentless assault on flesh that bore no visible trace of blood. She jerked a paper towel from the dispenser and using her knuckles, she scrubbed so hard her skin blossomed scarlet red.

Lifting his vision, he saw her anguish in the mirror as she feverishly worked. She was crying again.

The brutal scouring she gave herself sent a shiver down his spine. At that rate, she'd scrub to the bone. He covered her hand with his, stopping her. She left no question how she felt about it either, "I have to get the blood off. It's the only way."

"Let me do it," he said and not as a request. He soaped her arms then turned the cold water on to temper the full-out steaming hot water she'd used. He rinsed her arms and gently dried them. A quick glance revealed she scarcely held herself in check as more tears welled in her eyes. The image broke his heart, "It's been a bad night but we'll get through this."

Tired sadness passed over her features, "I lied to her. I told her she'd be alright and I knew she was dying."

Ennis reached for the towel dispenser. He wetted the paper towel, soaped it up then brushed it over a stain of blood above her left breast, careful not to apply much pressure. He thought about the diagnosis and when the doctor might call. Aside from his mother, Savannah remained the strongest woman he'd ever seen. And, like his mother, when life presented an enormous challenge topped with a devastating event, she tended to bend under the pressure. Once Savannah regained her bearings, she'd jump into the saddle again like his mama did when his daddy passed on. It took a fair amount of time and loads of support from family, both of which his wife had, if she took advantage of it.

"You saved that girl from burning to death," he corrected. "And what if you'd been caught in that fire? Did you think how it would affect me?"

He evidently hit a poetic nerve with his last question. Tears slipped down her cheeks, "I was afraid that happened to you. I saw that fire flare up and I couldn't see you. I can't deal with the thought of losing you, Ennis. It's worried me ever since your shooting."

Ennis placed a kiss to her trembling lips, "I'm here for you now and always, you know that. I'm not gonna do something foolish and die. Now sit still and I'll be back."

He rounded the row of lockers in the center of the room. Her locker was easy to find with Lindsey's drawing taped to the door. Their niece depicted a female police officer with a ponytail standing in front of what was intended to be their station. The smiling character had her hands on her hips – a characteristic of Savannah's that Lindsey found endearing. If one looked closer, the nameplate on the uniform read "Prince". The picture always inspired a smile from Ennis.

From memory, he twirled the combination lock to and fro until it opened. He grabbed her spare blouse and jacket from inside. The rust pullover and beige colored jacket would go with her dark slacks, he guessed. Knowing Savannah, she'd insist on changing her slacks too. She'd called him colorblind ever since he tried wearing a canary yellow shirt with a light blue suit. "Runnin' off to join the circus?" she'd hinted.

Longing for such simplistic problems instead of the substantial load they currently carried, Ennis smiled at the recollection. On a lark, he grabbed the pair of slacks inside the locker. If she changed, fine. If not, it was easy enough to hang them back.

He eased around the corner to see her drying herself off. He slipped the rust blouse on her and took the opportunity to give her a peck on the lips, "There. That's better. Got your slacks too, if you want 'em."

She thanked him and when he stepped behind her and wrapped his arms around her, he felt her relax. She still shivered occasionally and that only encouraged him to draw her against him to warm and settle her.

"Ennis, I'm seriously considering putting in my papers. I'd..." she drew a shaky breath, "I'd like you to consider the same."

Ennis glanced down to ensure he had the right woman in his arms. Savannah Prince retire from the police department? The concept stunned him more than if she'd announced she wanted a dozen babies. "What?" was all he managed.

"Maybe Daddy was right. Maybe I need to concentrate on the orchards. He said I'd be good at helping manage them."

Ennis found it difficult to imagine R.J. Prince being right about anything. His observation showed the old man could occasionally rub two brain cells together and come out talking good sense. Savannah had brilliant bookkeeping abilities. She paid attention to detail the way Michelangelo labored over each brushstroke. R.J. was right but did she really want to dedicate her life to managing fruit and pecan orchards?

Mildly entertaining her request, he allowed his mind to wander into the forbidden. He easily pictured Savannah with a passel of kids and a minivan. He envisioned her attacking the job of PTA meetings with the passion she put into detective work. Warming his heart were images of his kids playing in a big backyard with a swing and swimming pool. He could see his son and daughter playing hide and seek with Lindsey and Dylan. He longed to spend Christmases with kids all around, every one of them Rutherfords and Princes. The fantasy wasn't all his own.

They discussed kids and it surprised him that she seemed receptive to the idea.

Before the biopsy, only one major hurdle stood in their way – her job. Chances were the night's events nudged her to the panic stage but by start of shift Monday she'd be ready for another case or bulling her way through a current one. He chose to hedge his answer, "Sugar, we'll talk about the job later. Tonight's not the best time to make life decisions."

Turning in his embrace, she wrapped her arms around him and held to him with a fierce strength. It reminded him of a drowning person. She clung with an intensity that threatened to drag them both under.

She nodded against his chest, "Just think about it, okay?"

Ennis hugged her tighter, "I promise." He slid a hand down her back, patted her bottom, "Once I locate our car, I'll meet you at Georgia's. I've been craving a piece of that peach pie – if you'll share it."

"Only with you," she said with a weary half-smile.

That eased his concern somewhat about her frame of mind. Even though the night still wore heavy in her mind, at least her personality began emerging again. That alone made him return the grin.

Savannah stepped from his embrace and went to her locker while he unlocked his. Sneaking a peek, he saw her changing her slacks and his smile widened. She slowly returned to her normal self which meant color coordination was essential. The black slacks ended up in a sack along with the matching jacket and the stained pink pullover. Ennis suspected she'd pitch it out once they arrived home.

She closed the locker with a subdued slam then rounded the corner, "Give me about thirty minutes to break the news about the biopsy then you can call your mother and tell her."

"If you want to wait, we can tell Georgia together."

She didn't immediately reply so he busied himself with changing his shirt. Savannah shook her head, "I'd better break the news myself. I appreciate the offer but…" her hesitation told him she struggled for the appropriate words. He was right, "That particular disease runs in the family. My maternal grandmother, my aunt and cousin on my mother's side had it too. Only one to catch it in time was my cousin and she…" Her words trailed off. She looked away but not before the color drained from her cheeks. With her silence, Ennis saw her reliving the memory in her mind.

"She went through a lot to survive it," was all she said.

One mystery about Savannah he never solved: how her mother passed away. Over the years he hinted and all but coerced her to discuss it. She'd shared the information about her father's physical abuse, her bad relationships with men, and various other private matters with him but never once alluded to how Charlene died. The current situation helped Ennis piece the puzzle together. Savannah mentioned her maternal grandmother, an aunt and cousin. Her distant behavior and moodiness the past few days explained more than she thought.

Savannah seemed to sense he now understood her fear, "Everything changes when you say it out loud, you know? And with this coming up, I have to convince Georgia to get checked too. She's six years older than me and with our history she's more vulnerable to it."

For the first time, Ennis realized how scared she was, no matter how calm she acted. He touched her cheek. She tilted into his palm, her eyes closed and she sighed.

The word "gentle" never came to mind for a man with his height and broad shoulders. Even his hands gave the impression of brute strength yet when his warm fingers touched her cheek, the delicate caress soothed her. Embracing him was like hugging a tree, solid and steady. When his arms enfolded her, she didn't just feel safe, she knew she was.

Being five feet nine, Savannah never looked petite like her sister. And unlike Georgia, her shoulders were slightly wider and it added to her critical self image. While men rallied around "little lady" Georgia, the same men regarded Savannah with caution thanks to her height and build. Georgia epitomized the Southern Belle without effort or intention. That was just her demeanor. She wasn't helpless nor cared to be seen as such. The men, seeing her graceful figure and beauty, assumed it so they flocked to her.

Savannah knew she wasn't striking like her sister. She didn't blame Georgia. She couldn't exactly help the fact she replicated their mother to the nth degree. More than once Charlene had the pleasure of being compared to Rita Hayworth. As a result, most men preferred Georgia over Savannah's "pretty" features. Of her mother's, nature gifted Savannah with the Hayworth-like smile that, according to Ennis, brought him to his knees.

Along with the smile, she favored her mother in other ways: her voice and bosom. Ennis called her voice "sultry" and supposedly loved to hear her talk. She found her husband endearing, if not strange at times. Because of her blunt nature, no man ever encouraged her to speak except him and that alone made her question his sanity.

Her bosom was average enough she didn't feel slighted in that department. Large breasts tended to attract men's attention and, depending on the male, would render them brainless and mute. For her job, that spelled trouble. She never thought about her boobs until she met Ennis. What once seemed irrelevant became an obsession. Not once did he look at them and the surprising part – she *wanted him to*. His vision remained above the neckline at all times and despite a few blushes here and there, he appeared uninterested in her bust. It drove her crazy. Were they too small? Were they uneven, misshapen or so abnormal he couldn't bear to look at them? Why the hell did she want him looking at them anyway, for God's sake? She'd slap any other man hard enough his tongue wrapped around his neck and strangled him. The fact Ennis Rutherford apparently never noticed her bosom disheartened her to the point she fixated over it.

Then, after their marriage, she couldn't keep him away from them. Along with his preoccupation with her hair, her two little friends became his as well. He'd noticed them all along, he confessed later, but, "My mama would beat me with a broom if she caught me lookin', at least until you and I were properly wed."

Since her doctor's appointment, she spent a lot of time staring at her left breast. If she had cancer, would Ennis change toward her like R.J. had Charlene? Would he distance himself from her, not touch her there again? Would they drift apart like her parents had? Common sense told her no but the doubt remained, however small. She knew she loved

Ennis more than life itself. Losing him equaled losing herself.

When he fell victim to a gunshot wound in the spring and nearly died, her love for him overrode her hatred for God. She prayed for him to live when, in her heart, she never believed prayer worked. After a long, arduous struggle, Ennis not only pulled through and returned to active duty, he eased her into accepting God again, to let go of her rage for her mother dying.

Savannah never told Ennis about Charlene's breast cancer. She elected to leave it at "an extended illness". Remembering how her mother suffered during her last days, Savannah finally realized God ended her pain. It devastated her to lose Charlene but watching her struggle to live while the cancer ravaged her body proved much harder. While her mother fought the cancer, Savannah battled her own war to deal with the impending loss. Before leaving for the hospital to visit Charlene, she made sure to swallow just enough courage to face her mother. Just enough proved to be her downfall when her cousin Bobby caught her fortifying herself before leaving his house. He blocked the exit and refused to let her leave. She tried pushing past him but his hands braced her with the solidity of a brick wall and he told her to sit down.

She didn't. Worse, she dared him to make her sit. She soon discovered her cousin possessed an unpleasant temper when provoked. He literally grabbed her by the arm and hauled her to the shower. He tossed her in the cold spray, startling her to temporary semi-sobriety.

Even while pitching a drunken fit, she realized she was no match for Bobby Prince who was ten years her senior and built as sturdy as the Atlanta Falcons' defensive line. It still didn't stop her from releasing her fiery temper. Her venomous words slid off her cousin like the shower's icy water poured off her. Bobby stood guard at the shower, watching her struggle to her knees then shoved her back down, "When you realize what you're doin' to yourself, *then* I'll let you out."

Savannah cursed him in ways that embarrassed her to that day. When she finished hurling expletives, sorrow overcame her. The reality of her mother's illness and her eventual passing ripped past her heart to her soul. She couldn't lose her mother, she sobbed. She couldn't *cope* with losing her.

With the physical battle over, Bobby settled next to the tub, his voice soft, "It'll be hard. For you and Georgia, it'll be the hardest thing you ever do 'cause you love her so much. But you don't want her passing on with this image of you, that you're an alcoholic like your daddy."

Clarity hit her like clouds parting after a storm. No, she didn't want her mother to pass away with that image. She tried her whole life to make her mother proud and had, at least according to Charlene. To see her youngest mired down in a bottle would break her heart. Trembling from the pelting bitter spray, Savannah pleaded with her cousin, "Take me to the hospital, Bobby. I need to tell Mama I'm not gonna drink anymore. I'll never take another drink..." She had, of course. After Charlene passed, Savannah reasoned her mother couldn't actually see her drink or know she had. And, as long as she stayed away from Bobby when she drank, who the hell cared? For Bobby's information, she was *nothing* like R.J. – nothing like him at all. She consumed just enough to cope with losing her mother. Just enough…

Now, clinging to Ennis for emotional stability, she wanted one drink. One small, teensy-weensie swallow to calm her nerves. She wouldn't turn into a swilling drunk, she promised herself, mostly because she didn't want Bobby tossing her in another cold shower.

That's when Elvis decided an interruption was in order. Her cell phone rang again with the familiar tune of "A Little Less Conversation". Savannah figured it was her sister calling again but glancing at the Caller ID revealed the name she expected to see all night. The culmination of the doctor's visits and the worry and dread sat in her hand, waiting to be revealed. Her heart refused to stop hammering in her chest. It pounded against her ribs with a force reminiscent of times she'd stared down the barrel of a loaded weapon. The possibility of dying at someone else's hand brought life into perspective. So did a much anticipated call from a doctor... "It's Dr. Wyatt," she said. Her voice didn't sound right. Damn, she sounded like a terrified kid. If that wasn't bad enough, she felt dizzy and in that short amount of time she'd begun to perspire. *Oh God*, she bemoaned, *I can't even cope with a phone call so how am I going to survive this news?*

Evidently sensing her weakness, Ennis tightened his hold. He eased her onto the bench in front of the locker, "Put it on speakerphone. We'll hear it together."

Her hands shook. Her thumb punched the speaker button and the phone teetered in her wobbly grasp. Ennis's hand covered hers, steadied the phone. He pressed a kiss to her temple, whispering, "Calm down."

Past the formal greetings, the doctor apologized for the late hour, "I promise I hadn't forgotten to call. Things were incredibly busy today and it's the first opportunity I've had."

"It's okay," she relieved him of his guilt though a scrap of resentment lingered. "Just glad you got a chance to call." Making people wait for test results constituted cruel and unusual punishment. So far she'd worried herself into a nervous breakdown, pissed off her husband and seriously considered driving to Wyatt's office and wringing the results from him with her bare hands. None of it mattered now. All she needed to know was, "So it's good news?"

The subsequent pause lasted forever. Dr. Wyatt stalled better than a Corvair but instinctively she'd known the truth all week. With her family history, the fact she didn't do self-exams or regularly go in for mammograms, it all added up to trouble.

Savannah leaned into Ennis, her hand reached for his. The gravity of the silence sank in. Doctors never paused with positive news. She concentrated on her husband's hold instead of Dr. Wyatt's imminent reply. Ennis's long, burly fingers were warm against her cold, trembling ones. He intuitively clasped her hand tighter. She took her cue from the doctor's hesitation, "It's not good news, is it?"

The doctor's voice surfaced from the small speaker, his tone contrite, "We need to schedule surgery. The biopsy came back malignant. I'm sorry, Savannah."

Her heart stopped the incessant hammering. It came to a brief complete halt then squeezed in her chest, making her cringe. Carefully planned words died on her tongue. She'd had questions to ask, things to say and they all vanished. Replacing them were memories of Charlene's diagnosis. She battled them back, pushed them to the recesses of her mind as she realized Ennis's hand was shaking. The "why me" and "why us" questions fighting to the forefront gave way to a prayer. *Help me be strong for Ennis.* Men were always the rocks for their wives. The good ones were, at least. When the man loved his wife with the intensity Ennis loved her, the news struck with the same impact. Savannah repeated her prayer, knowing Ennis needed her love and support as she needed his and only God could provide her strength to sustain them both.

Ennis curled his arm around her shoulders and drew her to him. "I'm here, sugar," he assured, his voice steadier than his hold. "We're in this together."

His embrace promised stability in her chaotic world. His voice pledged abiding love and support. She loved him more than anything and it wasn't just her health or life she feared losing most of all. She feared losing Ennis. Few men saw their wives through such a difficult situation. A lot of men left or divorced the wife, leaving her to cope alone. R.J. chose to cleverly souse himself in scotch to avoid the harsh reality. He provided no support for Charlene past being a warm body in her room while she died.

Scenes from that time trickled into Savannah's mind. The doctor assured Charlene the tumor was small, manageable and hadn't spread. In reality, he misdiagnosed the tumor and misjudged the severity of her situation. Georgia and Savannah begged their mother to seek a second opinion. By the time she had, it was too late.

Ennis pressed a soft kiss to her temple, mercifully dragging her from the haunting memories. Physically, she felt fine. Somewhat tired but she blamed it on the holiday and long hours associated with it. Surely Dr. Wyatt made a mistake – confused her results with some other unfortunate woman's. Cancer wasn't Savannah's worst fear. *Breast* cancer was. "Are you sure about the results?" she asked with a shred of hope in her voice. "I mean, it could be somebody else…"

Dr. Wyatt didn't hesitate this time, "I'm sure, Savannah. The tumor is relatively small but we do need to discuss surgical options as soon as possible."

Ennis spoke next, "What options are there?"

"Judging from the results, I'd recommend a lumpectomy with radiation treatments for five to six weeks. Some women in Savannah's position opt for a more radical approach to avoid radiation."

"In her position?" Ennis said, confused.

Savannah, though, understood the doctor's meaning. She just hadn't the heart to tell Ennis. Instead, she let Dr. Wyatt explain, "Her job requires a certain amount of activity and radiation can cause severe fatigue. The other possible side effects could hinder her abilities to perform at the level she does now. Some women choose to forego the radiation."

"How?" Ennis's frustration mounted.

Whether Wyatt lacked the fortitude to clarify, Savannah refused to guess. She only knew her husband's irritation escalated to anger. To save Wyatt the trouble and Ennis an eruption, she answered, "They have a mastectomy."

Along with his posture, Ennis's lungs deflated, leaving him as wilted as she'd felt for days. She chanced a look at him: his face, once a lively rosy color, now blanched lily white. His throat worked to either speak, swallow, or throw up, none of which he succeeded at. The weight and brutality of the disease penetrated his aggravation, replacing it with utter shock.

"Yes," the doctor concurred. "They're uncomfortable with a breast that's had cancer so they remove it."

The brief pause found her looking again to Ennis. His wide eyes hesitantly met hers with a question. Reading his mind was no challenge. He wanted to know if she considered the mastectomy option. A small shake of her head did little to ease the worry lines trenched deep between his coffee brown eyes.

Wyatt went on, "In fact, some women choose to have a double mastectomy..."

And that's where Savannah finally heard Ennis take a breath. A long, gasping breath that reminded her of Lindsey's reaction when Dylan stuck a frog in her face. To calm Ennis down, Savannah voiced her preference, "I'd rather not entertain those alternatives until I have to."

Until then her husband's painful grasp hadn't registered. Ennis gripped her hand so hard the bones hurt. Once she expressed her opinion, the hold slackened a few degrees to a manageable one. Savannah breathed a sigh of relief and her hand felt particularly grateful.

"I understand completely," Wyatt acknowledged. "As I said, at this point I prefer the lumpectomy with radiation. During the surgery I can make a better determination. Since the tumor looks small, I'll remove some surrounding tissue for insurance and also take a sentinel node biopsy. We'll test the sample to see if the tumor has spread. I know it's a lot of information at one time so come in Monday and we'll review everything."

Now she just wanted the conversation to end, "What time?"

"Early as possible. Eight thirty sound good?"

"I'll be there," she agreed.

"No," Ennis corrected, "*we'll* be there."

After disconnecting the call, Savannah stared at the phone. A hundred different thoughts raced through her already cluttered mind. She ran a hand through her hair and sighed. Her future just took a staggering unforeseen turn. At best was surgery followed by radiation then recovery. At worst was surgery, chemo then a funeral...

As if he sensed her thoughts, Ennis tightened his hold again. A bolt of pain shot up her arm and when she looked up, tears glistened in her husband's eyes. He hadn't tried to break her train of thought, he tried to maintain his composure.

She grabbed him in a hug, "Ennis, it'll be okay. He said it's small." *They said that about Mama's too*, her mind taunted. Pushing the voice away, she concentrated on calming her husband. Most times he presented a steel exterior, a rock for her to cling to in turbulent times. This time, she realized, it was her turn to toughen up and be *his* rock.

Ennis constricted his hold. Savannah hadn't experienced an embrace that intense since Mama Rutherford welcomed her to the family. "Ennis," she started only to have the air literally squeezed from her. "It'll be okay," she whispered with what breath remained.

A noise behind the lockers drew her attention. Obviously realizing their blunder, the person, whoever it was, stood stone still. Dealing privately with the news would be hard enough but the idea of a co-worker knowing her condition would present a unique form of hell. She'd planned to tell their captain in her own time, not have it spread through the stationhouse by a nosy eavesdropper. During the call, neither of them considered guarding the door to prevent such things. She assumed their meddlesome companion overheard the entire conversation. "Who's there?" she demanded.

Footsteps shuffled along the floor. A chubby stomach wrapped in a buttoned suit coat came into view then John Mathis peeked around the corner, his hands raised in surrender, "I wasn't listening in, I swear."

Savannah's anger ebbed and thunderous heartbeat settled to a normal rhythm. If anyone at the station had to find out, besides their captain, John Mathis was probably safest. They'd been friends for years and shared parts of their lives that no one else was privy too. Mathis also attended hers and Ennis's wedding – another little secret that no one spoke of. Two detectives in the same station getting married wasn't forbidden but if those detectives were partners, it was. Mathis promised to keep his mouth shut and Savannah trusted him to. Now she needed to trust him with another important secret.

Her fellow detective averted his gaze, "I heard about your..." For the first time since she'd known him, John Mathis stumbled for words. He tried again, "Your condition and all. If there's anything I can do, let me know, will ya?"

She nodded, wondering if Ennis ever planned to let go. Probably considered stifling by most people, she found the embrace comforting even as a few bones popped into realignment. Truthfully, she didn't want him to let go. She wanted to stay in his arms forever, no matter how blue she turned from oxygen deprivation.

Mathis stood, seemingly as overwhelmed as they were. Savannah wasn't sure how long her brave front might hold. She never accepted change well. Considering it involved her health, she doubted her demeanor would improve. For Ennis, though, she wanted to keep her poise as long as possible. Telling Mathis to clam up need not be said but Ennis didn't share the many years of friendship with him she did. Before her husband blurted something less than tactful, Savannah voiced a gentle reminder, "John, I'd appreciate it if you'd keep this to yourself. I'll tell the boss this weekend."

John stared at the floor, "Yeah, no prob," he replied quietly. "But let me know when the surgery is."

Again she nodded. Mathis placed a hand on her shoulder, the other on Ennis's, "Guys, my sister had it and they did surgery and chemo. She's still running around aggravatin' me worse than ever and it's been nine years now." After a squeeze, he added, "You got a lot of people on your side, me included."

Normally, Mathis never had to worry about winning any diplomacy awards, especially on the job. With one look, he managed to alienate witnesses and suspects alike. But at that moment, Mathis proved to Ennis something Savannah already knew. Their rough-around-the-edges colleague really did have a heart.

6

They parted ways at the police station with Ennis on a mission to locate their detective's car. Savannah decided to head out to Georgia's and inform her of the week's events. All Georgia needed was the information, not details and considering Savannah was devoid of those anyway, the conversation promised to be short.

On the way to her sister's house, Savannah's mind wandered to her future. While a drastic measure, retiring from the department seemed a reasonable decision plus it would thrill Lindsey to no end. She sensed Ennis's skepticism when she mentioned it. He obviously failed to recognize her inability to detach anymore. She'd seen too much, witnessed too many painful things in her career. Between Hayley's death and Dr. Wyatt's phone call, the night not only left her devastated and depressed, it practically finished her off.

Cops were held to an impossible standard. They were expected to be everywhere and protect everyone. They did their best but inevitably screwed up somewhere, somehow. Assessing her career, she concluded that only a machine (and the chief) could calculate the number of her blunders. Her commendations proved she made *some* decent decisions but when she screwed up, she made it count. She expected the paramedics to contact her boss concerning her conduct. Whatever Josh Hunter decided to do, she'd accept. Hell, life threw her the granddaddy of curveballs – which she failed to duck – so anything short of dismissing her would be pretty insignificant. She admitted to losing her temper with the paramedics. No, she took that back. For a few brief minutes, she'd lost her *mind*. Before she lost it forever, she needed to analyze her life. Depending on her diagnosis and the outcome, her career dangled in the balance anyway.

The more she mulled over retiring, the more appealing it grew. She and Ennis would have time together for other things. Things most married couples enjoyed – couples whose jobs had normal hours instead of the nightly marathons they tended to have. Surviving on coffee, candy bars and various forms of caffeine got old quick. If they lived a normal existence, they could think about having children, if her illness and treatment didn't delay them or prevent them from having kids at all.

The possibility of never having kids brought forth the sincere urge to drink again. One trip to the package store – the first in ten years – no one could hold that against her, or at least they'd better not try. On that grim note, she added the realization she could mentally map out most of the liquor stores within her working and living radius. She clenched her teeth. *I'm not like Daddy. I haven't had a drink in ten long years. I never truly wanted one until now...* She winced at the last statement. It was a lie. She craved the bottle when Ennis was shot. She tried to drink – even had the bottle in her hand – only for the troops to rally against her. Some, like Dane, encouraged her not to drink while her siblings outright threatened her if she did. When they sicced Lindsey on her, the youngster succeeded on leveling the mother of all guilt trips on her. It was difficult to get sloshed in front of a kid who, according to Seth, considered her a role model.

She hadn't confessed to Ennis about her past with alcohol. Knowing Dane or any of her snoopy relatives, she figured he already knew or suspected it anyway. Her steadfast refusal to drink one drop probably signaled a fanaticism about drinking or someone battling a private war. One thing about her husband – he wasn't the typical male she was accustomed to. Her husband's keen sixth sense tended to spook her. He picked up on certain words, mannerisms and her actions with a skill she never expected or encountered in a man. His perceptiveness surpassed Georgia's and rated up there with Charlene's so telling him about her earlier struggle with the bottle probably would be met with a nod, a hug and a "glad you finally told me".

She opted to drop by Cheers Package Store along Forsyth. One or two swallows provided enough solace to last the evening. She only needed enough to survive Christmas…

For some reason her father assumed she couldn't handle liquor because she retched at the smell of scotch. She wanted to tell him she could handle any liquor *except* scotch. Her drink of choice was bourbon. It was heavier than scotch but to her it was smoother, richer and worked faster. And as for Georgia's brandy, a good bourbon made it look unequivocally namby-pamby. For Savannah, drinking brandy was like waiting in line at the DMV. It took too long to get the job done.

Her foot pressed the accelerator to expedite her arrival at Cheers. Driving down Forsyth, she approached the Greyhound terminal and was about to turn toward Cheers when a flash of pink caught her eye. Doing a double-take, she saw a little girl standing outside the bus station. The child's vision searched the crowd around her, her face uncertain, even slightly scared. She looked about five or six years old, Savannah thought as she slowed and pulled to the curb. The girl looked overwhelmed in the rush of people scurrying past. She stepped out of the throng's path, one lilac mitten-clad hand clutched a small Barbie suitcase, the other gathered her pink coat's collar at her neck.

It seemed she looked for someone in particular and as the crowd thinned to a few stragglers, she resigned herself to huddling against the terminal's brick wall.

Savannah watched to see if she went inside to the safety and warmth of the building. She didn't.

Suddenly the trip to the package store went on hold. First she'd tend to the little girl then hurriedly visit Cheers then beat it to Georgia's before her sister's mood took a nosedive. Georgia missed Dane who was back in Texas for the holiday. He'd invited Georgia along but she bowed out without giving explanation. Though her sister missed her sweetheart, after the night's events and the diagnosis, Savannah was grateful Georgia stayed behind. Next year, she expected the two to wed and probably have a little one on the way. But this Christmas, Georgia sank into a reflective, sullen mood and dealt with it the only way she knew how. She cooked. God only knew how much food Georgia prepared but Savannah braced herself for a feast large enough to feed a small country.

Watching the youngster pull the lilac colored stocking cap further over her long brown hair, Savannah wondered how she managed the cold so well. For the first time in years, Atlanta found itself encased in a dense frigidity that had residents and tourists alike huddling indoors. Snow continued drifting down from the heavens, coating sidewalks, cars and grass. If the child meant to hang out in an icebox, she chose the perfect location. Savannah shook her head. She had to convince the child to go inside and explain the dangers if she didn't. Number One, she'd catch her death. Number Two, Savannah would bet her next paycheck she wasn't the only one watching the youngster from afar.

It was nine by the car's clock and only streetlights and the Greyhound sign brightened Forsyth Street. Nighttime – the best time for criminals to strike and a cute kid by herself was, perhaps, the most tempting target.

The girl had to be freezing and whoever promised to pick her up either didn't realize the temperature and time of day or possibly just didn't care. Savannah eased the red Camaro across the intersection and parked at the corner. She rolled the window down and called to the girl, "You alone, sweetie?"

The child glanced in her direction then buried her chin back in her coat collar like a retreating turtle. Savannah smiled. *Don't talk to strangers.* Her parents and siblings instilled that warning at an early age too. She retrieved her badge, holding it for the girl to see, "I'm with the police, sweetheart. If you're waiting for someone to pick you up, I'd feel better if you went inside the bus terminal. It's warmer and safer in there."

The little girl shook her head and clutched the small suitcase closer. Savannah rolled the window up and killed the engine. She got out and rounded the front of the Camaro, her tone soft, "Well, I can't let you stand out here all alone. I can call someone for you, drop you off at their house or stay with you until that person arrives."

She spoke through the coat's thick collar, "No one's coming. I don't know anyone here."

Savannah's brow furrowed. No one? Well, she knew one thing for sure. She wasn't about to leave the child by herself. It didn't take a genius to realize the danger in doing so. Savannah decided to take it one step at a time, "Well, you know *me*." She bent down and extended her hand, "I'm Savannah."

The girl stared at the outreached hand then lifted her vision to Savannah's, sizing her up. From the minimal amount of the girl's face peeking over the coat's collar, Savannah could tell she had pretty green eyes. The youngster slid a small hand into hers, "Hi, Savannah. I'm Emily."

"That's a pretty name. You know, Emily, it's awful cold out here. Why don't we go inside and get some hot chocolate?"

She shook her head, "I'm scared of those places. Too many people."

Savannah understood completely. Bus terminals, airports and places bogged down with people drove her to practically scream and the holidays were the worst. Swarms of noisy people scrambling to get one place or another, Savannah could imagine how frightening it was for a child alone – not only in the mix but in a strange city. "May I ask why you're traveling alone?"

Emily huddled down in the coat until, "I'm going to see Daddy for Christmas. He lives in Memphis. Mama stayed home 'cause she had to work."

By this time, Savannah crouched to one knee to cut the wind off her. Wearing the suit jacket provided minimal protection from the bitter wind. More than once that day she bemoaned the fact she neglected to bring an actual coat along. She rubbed her arms and Emily saw it, "You should get back in your car. I'll be okay."

Savannah shook her head, her tone thoughtful, "I told you I can't leave you here by yourself. Say, have you had supper yet?"

Emily shook her head again. Savannah asked when the girl's bus departed.

"They said eleven," she answered.

"My sister is cooking a swell Christmas Eve meal right now and it's only going to be a few of us there. Why don't you eat supper with us and I'll make sure you get back here for your next ride?" She saw Emily weighing the offer and added, "She's promised me a peach pie *and* Triple Chocolate Cake for dessert and I'll bet an extra piece would come in handy on your trip."

"Can I see your badge again?"

The question threw Savannah temporarily but she withdrew the badge and I.D. from her jacket pocket. Emily studied it thoroughly and after a moment Savannah retrieved her cell phone, "Want to call my captain to verify I'm a police officer?"

Emily's vision bounced up to find the playful grin on Savannah's face. A tiny smile surfaced behind the coat, "I trust you." Then the smile disappeared, "Won't your sister be inconvenienced by me being there? She's only preparing so much food."

Savannah's mouth opened to reply but stopped. The young child used the words "inconvenienced" and "preparing" as though she'd used them all her life. "Uh, not really. Georgia always fixes enough for a crew on a battleship. She'll be delighted to have another guest." Savannah stood and guided Emily to her car, "Hop in and we'll thaw you out."

The girl settled into the large bucket seat, her Barbie suitcase still in hand. She buckled up and finally seemed to relax once the initial blast of warm air circulated around her. Savannah heard her sigh and asked, "Feeling better now?"

Emily nodded. The longer they traveled, Savannah noted instead of roaming the neighborhood's Christmas displays, the girl's attention riveted on the silver angel dangling from the rear-view mirror. She lifted her chin from the coat's collar, her hand touched the angel, "It's beautiful."

For eleven years the angel swayed in the corner of Savannah's vision. She'd bought it as a connection to her mother. Over the years the gold ribbon faded to white and the silver peeled from the wings. Emily probably wanted an explanation of why she had the angel but Savannah wasn't interested in telling a painful tale on Christmas Eve, especially with the news she just received, "Thanks. It's been with me a long time."

Taking the answer at face value, Emily followed with, "It's really nice of you to do this."

Savannah made a turn and glanced at her small companion, "Are you kidding? We'll love having you there and my sister is crazy over kids so get ready to be spoiled."

Emily smiled a tiny smile. Savannah caught a glimpse that inspired one of her own to surface.

"What about your mama and daddy? Will they be there too?"

Savannah's smile faded. Her parents were not a favorite subject at Christmas. Not because she didn't love them but because of the heartache it presented. Growing up, her father, R.J., hadn't been easy to love. He enjoyed bars too much and enjoyed hitting people more, especially his children. She and Georgia were his only children to include R.J. in their Christmas festivities. Most times he bowed out or ignored the invite. This year, Savannah hoped he'd bow out. R.J. perfected the art of ruining holidays with his boisterous, sometimes hateful opinions, fabricated grudges and drunken ravings.

Since Charlene passed away, the profound loss seemed to grow over the years. They stretched longer and more difficult and even after eleven years, she could hardly mention her mother at the holidays. Georgia either felt the same way or sensed how much talking about Charlene hurt Savannah so she didn't mention her either.

Savannah blinked back tears and from the corner of her eye saw a small hand reaching for her. Emily grasped her hand, the small cool fingers clasped her palm and for some inexplicable reason, Savannah found comfort in the hold.

"I'm sorry, Savannah."

Impulse nearly slammed Savannah's foot on the brake. That voice. She knew that voice because she'd grown up with it and it didn't belong to a little girl. The rich, gentle tone with a hint of Georgia brogue belonged to her mother. She cut her vision to the side. No, the voice didn't come from Emily but she swore she heard her mother's voice. Savannah purposefully blinked once then twice in an attempt to align her senses. *I've had a long week and a bad night,* she thought, *but I didn't think I was completely losing my mind too.* She assured herself she hadn't actually heard Charlene's voice – that she missed her mother and *wanted* to hear her voice.

"I didn't mean to upset you," Emily's young voice said.

"Tonight's just a bad night. Next to my mother passing away, it's the worst." The urge to drink again surfaced full force as it did on certain stressful occasions. Fighting it off sounded easier than it was. She hated imbibing for fear R.J.'s habit might trickle down to become hers as well. Plus, if she drank when she was depressed, she sank further until ugly, self-destructive thoughts took over.

"Christmas Eve is special, that's what Daddy says," Emily said quietly. "If you wish something, it might come true."

"The wishes I have can't come true. For one, I can't bring my mama back."

"She's with you, you know. In your heart."

Savannah refused to discuss the most painful memory of her life, even with a young stranger. She spent the last fifteen minutes giving herself a pep talk about Dr. Wyatt's phone call and trying to purge negative thoughts and feelings from her weary mind. The last thing she wanted to do was get into a philosophical conversation with a kid. Thankfully her cell phone rang, giving her mind something else to deal with other than vacating the premises. It was Georgia, "Daddy's not coming. He begged off until New Year's."

"And you're surprised?"

"What's wrong with *you?*"

Savannah sighed. She hadn't the time or energy to explain,

"Nothing, sorry. Listen, I'll be there in a few. I'm bringing a guest, okay?"

"Tall, dark and handsome and goes by the name Ennis Rutherford?"

"Not exactly. He's coming later. The guest I'm talking about is about six, female and dressed in pink. Her name is Emily."

There was a momentary silence then Georgia recovered, her voice retaining its cheerfulness, "It's definitely not who I expected you to bring but she'll brighten us all up, I'm sure. Kids always do."

7

The second Georgia opened the door, the aroma of baked ham wafted past. As a result, Savannah's stomach voiced its displeasure at waiting to devour the tasty meal. After sheepishly apologizing for the loud hunger pains, she drew Emily beside her and noticed the beaming grin on the kid's face as she looked up at Georgia. It didn't faze Savannah anymore. Kids took to Georgia like butterflies flocking to flowers.

When Savannah's vision lifted to her sister she found her pale, like she'd seen a ghost. Strangely Georgia's smile faded the moment she saw Emily. Savannah swore pure shock registered. "You look like…" Georgia began then abruptly closed her mouth. Unsure of what rattled her sister so, Savannah hesitantly introduced them. She watched Georgia, who'd mentally regrouped, bend down and extend her hand, "You look like you might be hungry. I hope you are because I prepared a rather large meal."

While Emily shook Georgia's hand, Savannah replied, "I forewarned her you only cook in quantity."

As Georgia gathered the girl inside, she addressed her sister, "Well, I was hoping Daddy might join us this year. You remember how he could inhale ham? That's why I bought a big one."

Savannah shrugged, "So send the girl a couple of sandwiches for her trip. By the way, I need to talk to you later. It's important..." Her original thought gave way to astonishment upon viewing the inside of Georgia's house. In the matter of a day, the place transformed from rich burgundy and hunter green elegance to Christmas green and red. Lights and tinsel adorned the front window where the Christmas tree sat and more lights hung from doorways and outlined the front door. Jesus and Santa figurines sat on the coffee table and Georgia's mahogany writing desk. Topping off the festive atmosphere, she'd draped boughs of garland along her stairway railing, complete with evenly spaced red bows.

Savannah couldn't believe her eyes, "My God, Georgia. What'd you do? Knock over the Christmas store in the mall?"

Perfectly proud of her efforts, Georgia answered, "I needed something to do."

"Your enthusiasm is frightening. I'd employ you to clean my house but I remember how thorough you are. I'd never find anything again." She shook her head, "You must have been Santa's elf in another life."

A gleeful Emily beamed, "Your house is beautiful."

Georgia chuckled then pleasantly jibed, "At least someone appreciates my work." She thanked Emily who wandered the living room, inspecting trinkets and photos sitting on Georgia's writing desk and coffee table. Emily's careful, studious manner drew both sisters into watching her roam, not touching anything but concentrating on the photos lining the edge of the desk.

Georgia saw her linger at their parent's wedding portrait and one of Georgia and Dane together. Her vision cut to Savannah, "So what's the story, anyway?"

Savannah gave her a brief run-down on how she'd met Emily. She finished about the time the girl offered, "Your husband is very handsome. You look perfect together."

Georgia blushed, "Thank you but we're just friends."

To that, Savannah snorted her doubt. Dane and Georgia spent more time together than two hibernating bears. Their behavior with each other suggested plenty more than friends. Just a few days earlier Savannah remarked to Ennis that the airlines were making a fortune off Dane Rutherford for all his traveling. It would be cheaper to get married and stay in one place.

Emily evidently sensed the same, "You look like you're in love."

Georgia, poised to reply, instead stood speechless at the statement. Savannah couldn't help but chuckle.

The girl touched the frame holding R.J.'s and Charlene's photo, "You both favor your mother."

They both thanked her but Savannah noticed Georgia was more guarded this time. Something, Savannah surmised, was definitely askew with her sister and it began the instant she saw Emily.

She elected to dodge Georgia's inquisitive appearance and get something to salve her own pain. After all, she hadn't gotten the chance to drop by the package store...

Savannah marched straight to Georgia's bottle of Metaxa Grande. Since she was old enough to drink, her sister preferred the Greek brandy. At a hundred bucks a bottle, it should have been liquid gold. Savannah believed it was a waste of money, that a middle-class or budget brandy would suffice. In the end, top-shelf or budget, they all did the same thing.

Savannah held no particular fondness for brandy but at the moment anything would help kill the emotional turmoil rolling in her mind. Memories and bad news. *Merry Christmas*, she mused dismally.

A hand on her wrist stopped her before she poured, "What's going on?" Georgia asked. "You never drink."

Well, that wasn't subtle at all, was it? Savannah noticed the emphasis on "you never drink" as though diplomatically reminding her not to. Setting the bottle down, she decided to ask – no matter how crazy she'd sound, she still had to know, "Have you ever…" She lowered her voice to a whisper, "Have you ever heard Mama talk to you?"

"Mama?" A puzzled frown emerged. "You haven't been drinking already, have you?"

"Cut it out," Savannah warned. "I'm serious. Have you ever heard Mama talk to you? I need to know."

Georgia took a deep breath, contemplated her answer. "After she passed, yes. Even years later I thought I heard her. What's all this about Mama anyway? You never talk about her at the holidays and from the looks of it," her vision dropped to the brandy, "it's a good thing." She wrapped her hand around the bottle's neck, reinforcing her refusal of a simple taste, "You don't want or need this."

She hated getting snippy with Georgia but, "Oh yeah? First of all, you haven't experienced my day. Second, you were listing to the whiter shade of pale the instant you saw Emily. Sure you don't want to join me for a swallow?"

"You called this flavored paint thinner the last time you drank it so I'm relatively positive it won't taste better now. You're upset and depressed and this only makes it worse, remember?"

Savannah pursed her lips to prevent herself from lashing out. *Not in front of the kid,* her mind cautioned. She wouldn't lose her composure in front of a child but having her past thrown at her like someone slinging shit didn't make her exactly happy. She remembered plenty about drinking. Foremost she recalled how it helped her temporarily forget her troubles. Tonight, "temporarily" sounded damn great.

She watched Emily go to the small, modest Christmas tree sitting in the front window. The multicolored twinkling lights illuminated the girl's features with an angelic glow.

Savannah's blue eyes narrowed at the scene, her mind still edgy but more perplexed than anything, "There's something about that kid. I don't know what. She's…" she searched for the appropriate term, "different." She tried dislodging the bottle from her sister's hold by finessing a gentle tug, "Ever since she mentioned Mama and Daddy being here tonight."

As expected, Georgia held firm to the brandy, "It's a natural assumption. You're just sensitive because you miss Mama. You can't hold that against the girl since she didn't know."

Her sister's condescending phraseology had Savannah close to yanking her own hair out, "I realize that, Georgia. You're missing my whole point. It's like she *knows* us but in my rational mind, I realize she *couldn't*."

Georgia sighed, no doubt feeling the severe tension building between them, "Honey, you've been working sixteen hour days for weeks. I don't see how you retain a rational mind at all. Do me a favor, okay? Eat supper and see if you feel any better. Then later, drop Emily off for her bus, come back and we'll all talk." She waited for her younger sister to surrender the brandy – which she begrudgingly did – then slipped her arm around Savannah's waist, "We've got each other and we don't need that silly bottle."

"Yeah. Mama at least wanted her kids sober so I'll try to give her that."

Georgia nodded, "She was a unique but strong woman. She still loved Daddy, even with his drinking problem."

"And hitting problem."

"Savannah," her sister gently scolded. "It's Christmas. Try to be nice."

8

The counters brimmed with a day's worth of baked dishes for Christmas Day when the sisters and Ennis would go to Seth's house for supper. Savannah knew by rote which dishes were taboo until Christmas Day. Georgia always split the Christmas Eve leftovers between herself, Savannah and Ennis and that was darn fine with Savannah. Her eyes practically glazed over at the sight of ham. It reminded her of Georgia's annual joke, "If you want Savannah's undivided attention, wave a ham sandwich or peach pie under her nose."

Besides the ham, Georgia prepared mashed potatoes and gravy, corn, homemade hot rolls and a passel of green beans seasoned lightly with onion. It was the image of that meal that kept Savannah semi-civil all week.

Christmas songs drifted from Georgia's stereo in the living room. It surprised Savannah since her sister never played music at the holidays. Hearing them, she kinda wished she'd not started it either. Her sister's taste in music differed greatly from hers. Savannah grooved to classic Christmas tunes from Gene Autry and Bing Crosby while Georgia settled into classical and operatic types. Teeth grinding music, Savannah called it. And at the current time, The Three Annoying Tenors wailed away at "Ave Maria". "Is that the radio?" she asked, knowing it wasn't.

"No," Georgia answered, particularly more inspired than her sister, "it's my new CD. Isn't it great?"

Savannah grabbed the bowl of mashed potatoes and tried not to flinch at the bellering shrieks in the other room, "Yeah, it's a gem." The "singers" reached octaves only dogs could detect, she'd bet money on it. And if the braying continued, she'd take to howling too, "You got any Chuck Berry or Supremes?"

Passing by with the homemade rolls, Georgia frowned, "'Fraid not. You don't like the music?"

Calling it "music" was a matter of opinion. But to avoid hard feelings, she conceded, "No, it's fine," as one of the Three First Sopranos began yowling his version of "Silent Night". *Sounds like a strangling cat...*

When she glanced to the living room, Emily's attention riveted to their conversation. She appeared entertained by the bantering so as Savannah sat the potatoes on the table, she winked at the girl, "How about the Beach Boys? Everyone loves 'Little Saint Nick'." She hummed a few bars just in case her sister lost her entire memory.

Georgia took the chiding in stride, "Honestly, there are times I don't know how Ennis stands your sense of humor."

"Indulgence mostly," Ennis replied. "But I'm partial to the Beach Boys too."

Georgia shook her head, "If there were any questions that you deserve each other, this settled it."

Emily giggled at the friendly teasing as the two sisters returned to the kitchen for more food. Savannah noticed the little girl's face brightened with a smile as Emily spoke with Ennis. In fact, she even blushed when Ennis complimented her. Savannah's heart ached watching her husband's inherent ability with kids. His effortless conversational knack put children at ease as evidenced by Lindsey and Dylan who took to him the instant they met him. Clearly so did Emily.

Surveying the scene at the dining table, Savannah touched her stomach, the yearning for kids surfacing again. Ennis would make an excellent father. It was her parenting skills that worried her. Sure, she was an okay aunt but her own kids? What happened if she screwed up and they ended up on America's Most Wanted later in life?

"Are you thinking about having kids?"

Georgia's intuitive nature unnerved her. Was her desire that obvious or was her sister clairvoyant? Savannah verbally backtracked but stumbled on her tongue instead. To end the ridiculous stammering, she settled for an awkward shrug.

"That's a first. At least you're not threatening to tar and feather me for mentioning that subject." Her sister smiled what Savannah considered a shrewd smile. God, she hated when Georgia read her mind. In years past, she'd argue with Georgia but today she hadn't the heart, especially since she was right.

Georgia plopped the bowl of green beans in her hands, "You'd make a good mom and you already know Ennis would be a great dad."

Savannah's vision lifted to hers, "I worry I'll royally mess up somehow."

A carefree laugh bubbled from the older sister, "Honey, *everyone* worries about that. Don't let your concern prevent you from trying."

A smile traveled halfway across Savannah's lips when the thought of breast cancer invaded once again. The smile waned, "I've really got to tell you something but it'll have to be later, after I get Emily back to the bus station."

Georgia appraised her expression. Savannah wasn't sure if her sister's innate perceptiveness kicked in or Georgia heard the slight desperation in her voice. Whatever the case, the eldest reclaimed the green beans, "Are you sure? We could delay supper a little longer." She peeked into the dining room, "They're in their own world anyway."

"Believe me, I need privacy for this," Savannah took back the green beans and sauntered into the dining room with a cheerful greeting.

Ennis and Emily's conversation ended on a laugh, and her husband pointedly made eye contact. Savannah read the question in them – did you tell Georgia yet – and she shook her head, "Later." She eased his frown by assuring, "I promise."

Emily beamed from ear to ear, "Ennis is a great guy."

Savannah rounded the table and kissed his cheek, "That's why I married him."

The child continued, "He's been telling me all about your plans."

Georgia brought up the rear with a platter of ham. She paused when she saw Savannah stop in mid-sit beside Ennis, the younger sister's vision shifting to her husband. Ennis surpassed any kid caught with his hand in the cookie jar. She felt his desire to look away but he couldn't. He squirmed instead.

"What plans?" Savannah asked. Along with the conversation, the tunes took a dire turn as longhair music floated into the room. Probably Bach, she lamented, and his Greatest Hits at that...

"You're retiring from the police and he's hoping for lots and lots of babies."

At that point, the music didn't matter because both Savannah and Georgia literally dropped into their chairs from utter shock, their jaws following suit by gaping open. The older sister managed to safely set the platter down before her rounded eyes met Savannah's, "Is this the news you wanted to tell me?" A smile formed at the corners of Georgia's mouth. Savannah saw the announcement spreading from her brain to her mouth with lightning speed. The first thing her brain said: Wait till I tell...

To avert any unpleasant conversation, Savannah shook her head with a grim, "That isn't my news."

Ennis shrank back, looked away. Savannah tried to ease his guilt about blabbing her perspective plan to a child they didn't even know, "I did mention retiring from the job and I also asked Ennis to entertain the thought as well. As for kids, we need more time to discuss it."

Georgia's upbeat mood never faltered. She offered a hand to her sister, the other to Emily, "Well, just hearing you say that makes this holiday more joyous. Having you both out of harm's way will make next Christmas even more special." She added a lilt to her voice, "And there's a little girl who'll be thrilled to hear it."

"Don't breathe a word to Lindsey. We're still discussing it."

"I won't tell. I'd love to see her reaction to the news though. In the meantime, let's say the prayer."

Savannah clasped her sister's hand and thought about next

Christmas… God only knew what it might bring. At the rate her life fell apart, she dreaded contemplating it too much.

In years past, Georgia said the prayer and expecting her to begin, Savannah bowed her head. Instead, Emily offered thanks, "Father, bless Savannah, Ennis and Georgia and their families. They've welcomed me into their lives like a friend when most people wouldn't. Lord, I ask a special blessing for Savannah. She's going through a troubled time and needs Your comfort and love…"

Halfway through, Savannah heard a change in the voice offering the prayer. She heard Charlene speaking, not a little girl, but she was afraid to open her eyes. She was truly afraid she was losing her mind. Savannah peeked over at Georgia who didn't seem to notice a change. *Oh my God*, Savannah thought, *I am going crazy.*

Ennis gently squeezed her hand when Emily reference "a troubled time" and that shifted her vision to him. Had he noticed a change in the girl's voice? By his calm demeanor, no, he hadn't. *I'm truly certifiable. I wonder if the department insurance covers mental breaks…*

"…embrace them all in Your loving arms, Father. In Your Name I pray, Amen."

Lifting her head, Georgia zeroed in on Savannah – the message Savannah received – *now I know what you mean. This kid is different.* Somehow, though, she didn't think Georgia knew *how* different Emily really was but at least reviewing her insurance policy took a backseat…

Georgia dabbed a tear with her napkin, "Thank you for that beautiful prayer, Emily. I've never heard such eloquence from someone so young."

Savannah turned to the girl, "How old are you again?"

Displaying the same infectious grin she had with Ennis, Emily replied, "Five."

Still, the sisters found themselves at a loss for words. For a long moment, even Ennis sat bewildered at the phrases and words the young girl used in prayer but said nothing.

Confusion passed over Georgia's features, "What troubled time is she talking about?"

Savannah closed her eyes and prayed her reply went over better than it had with Ennis, "I'll tell you later, I promise." She'd rather eat and approach the subject with a full stomach if possible.

Emily's eyes shined as they darted from one dish to another, "Everything looks wonderful and smells heavenly."

"She's right," Savannah agreed, instructing herself to ignore the word "heavenly". Who cared that a five year-old uttered the word? And it really didn't matter that Charlene used it frequently. It didn't matter at all, she reasoned unsuccessfully.

They began filling their plates, passing each dish down until it came to Emily. Savannah helped her with the heavy dishes and made sure she had plenty to eat and for the first several minutes, the group quieted down while they ate.

Savannah's breast began aching which dulled her appetite. Recollections of little Gary, the "good" boy, brought a brief sneer to her face. The brat would probably get his new bike or whatever he wanted from Santa but had she, Georgia or Seth acted out like Gary had, R.J. would have beaten them within an inch of death. Charlene would have taken a switch to them but not as harshly as R.J.. Their mother's hand was considerably more disciplinary instead of abusive. Either way, the offending kid would have kissed their wish list to Santa goodbye.

"You okay?" Ennis leaned to her ear and whispered. "Looks like you're hurting again."

She nodded, "I'll take something for it later."

"What's wrong?" Georgia asked, returning her fork to her plate. She put owls to shame with the supersonic hearing. Considering her taste in Christmas music, Savannah figured Georgia was tone and stone deaf. The honed in stare told her different.

"Just been a very draining night," Savannah hedged. "I'll tell you later," she reminded. She glanced around the table at the enormous spread, "It's an excellent meal but you cooked enough for the whole neighborhood, even if Daddy showed up. He was really foolish to cancel." She didn't say one more word or else she'd hurt Georgia. Her sister prepared all their father's favorite dishes with hopes *this* year he'd spend Christmas Eve with them. Had he shown up, it would have been the first Christmas Eve in eight years. Otherwise, he spent his holiday at Abbott's Bar in Augusta.

Georgia managed a sad smile, "I wanted to please him since he hasn't eaten with us in so long." Trying to hide the dejection in her voice, she shrugged, "Maybe next year."

"Maybe," Savannah agreed, realizing they stood a better chance of dining with Elvis. R.J. missed his only opportunity to dine with his daughters at Christmas – like he cared. Seth refused to allow their father in his house and tried his best to shield his children from him. Savannah understood the reasoning. Being beaten with everything from bare hands to tree limbs soured a person on introducing new victims to the same treatment.

She, Georgia and Ennis would eat at Georgia's on Christmas Eve, then join Seth and his family the next day for gifts and a fat, juicy turkey – another of her weaknesses. She loved the holidays for the delicious food and serene family gatherings. It seemed everyone drew a universal truce – at least Georgia and Seth did. Savannah didn't think Seth would ever allow their father to attend a family function. That's why Georgia worked hard to ensure R.J. had an invitation to her house for Christmas Eve.

Ennis saved the moment by announcing, "This is the best ham I've ever eaten. How'd you fix it?"

Savannah silently thanked her husband and gifted him with a tiny smile. Then she spied a crumb at the corner of his mouth and swept it away with her thumb. The motherly move didn't seem to bother him.

Since being partnered with Ennis, she discovered his talent for learning people. He'd learned talking about food was the best way to divert Georgia's mind from her troubles. Tonight was no different as she explained, "I used a glaze of maple syrup, brown sugar, apple juice and Dijon mustard. Do you really like it?"

Savannah answered while dabbing his chin with her napkin, "Well, he's wearing some home so it's safe to assume he does."

Georgia smiled and before she replied, the phone rang. Savannah finished off the last of her ham and mashed potatoes as her sister excused herself and headed toward the kitchen. The next disc began playing which gave her nerves a respite. Savannah recognized it as Irving Berlin's "White Christmas". Thank God for normal music, she sighed while looking the table over. They pretty much plowed through the meal. Georgia would be happy. Nothing pleased her more than empty dishes and full stomachs around her table.

A quick perusal showed Emily cleaned her plate. "You want more?" Savannah offered. "As you can see, there's plenty."

An impish grin crossed the girl's cheeks, "I'm waiting for chocolate cake. I love chocolate."

"A true Southern girl. Always demand your chocolate. It's your right as a woman."

Ennis reached for another piece of ham then another spoonful of potatoes. Savannah dabbed a napkin at the corners of her mouth, addressing the little girl, "I'll go grab you a slice."

"Are you having one too?" Emily asked.

"Just try and stop me. Hold on, I'll be right back." Savannah made her way to the kitchen but stopped in the doorway. Georgia stood stunned, the phone still in her hand. To Savannah, it meant one thing. Someone died. "What's wrong? Is it Daddy?"

Georgia's green eyes lifted to meet Savannah's blue ones, her voice barely a whisper, "That was Mama Rutherford. She told me about your diagnosis."

9

The stares drove Savannah beyond crazy. Since Mama's call, Georgia began staring at her in mute disbelief – or something. Whatever it was, the steady gaze irked Savannah enough she retreated to the kitchen for her peach pie. She leaned against the cabinet, sank the fork past the flaky latticework crust and into the juicy peaches. Upon first taste, her eyes closed and she moaned her delight.

The moment she opened her eyes, not just one but three sets of eyes fixed on her. Now she had them *all* staring at her. Damn it, what was up with them? Emily had wide-eyed wonder in her expression. Ennis hid a smile. Georgia just kept staring. Savannah finally realized her reaction was louder than she expected. Using her fork, she pointed to the saucer, "Excellent peach pie."

"Can I have a piece?" Emily asked.

"You sure can, sweetie. Georgia makes sinfully delicious peach pies. She uses our mother's recipe. Mama put chefs to shame, didn't she, Georgia?"

Still speechless, Georgia's stupor held strong. Savannah sat the saucer aside, her frustration blossoming, "What is it, Georgia? Am I growing another nose?"

The question slapped Georgia from the daze and she dabbed a tear from each eye. She rose from her seat, "I'm sorry. I'm still in shock, I guess." She wandered into the kitchen, leaving Ennis with Emily.

Savannah refilled her tea glass, added a few spoonfuls of sugar and stirred it. Her sister, bless her heart, was a Southern woman but one couldn't tell it by her tea. Savannah missed Grandma Culberson's iced tea. The older woman had her share of quirks but no one topped her perfectly sugared tea. "I've been in shock since Monday," Savannah stated.

"Why didn't you tell me sooner?"

"Not you too," she groaned. "I've been locked in a car with Ennis all night playing Twenty Questions."

"I'd have gone with you," Georgia sounded hurt.

Great. Just what she needed. More guilt. "When I went in, I thought I was perfectly healthy."

"I'm talking about the biopsy, Savannah. Ennis told me you went through it alone. I could have gone – "

"When did he tell you?"

"When you and Emily were talking earlier. He also told me about Hayley and the accident this evening."

Her beloved had been rather busy. While she and Emily shared theories on how reindeer could fly, Ennis chatted Georgia up about Savannah's evening without her knowledge – or approval. She'd wanted to save her older sister the painful images of the wreck. Thanks to Ennis and his good intentions, Georgia knew it all. "I wish he hadn't done that," was all she said.

"He said you were pretty upset and justifiably so. He's concerned about you."

Savannah took a long sip from the glass, "I'll be fine."

Georgia busied herself wiping the cabinet tops with a dishrag, "He said you blamed yourself for Hayley's death."

Her irritation flared and before she threw the tea glass across the room, she sat it down, "You two pick the worst subjects to discuss." She lowered her voice in respect of the girl in the next room, "What happened to Santa, Rudolph, Jingle Bells and shit like that? We've got plenty of relatives to choose from so stop talking about *me*."

A frown darkened Georgia's features, "But you're the one in trouble. You stonewall everyone when you have a problem."

Savannah rubbed her forehead. Here it came. The time when Older Sister slipped into her Mama shoes to take the world over, or more to the point, *Savannah's* world. Georgia smothered her, R.J. berated her and Seth chose to ignore problems. And none of them understood why she withdrew at the first sign of trouble.

Georgia continued, "Ennis is afraid you'll need extra help coping with everything that's happened. You have to admit it's a tremendous load and it would help if you'd allow us to support you…"

As her sister babbled on, Savannah's brain locked up at the word "help". This sounded too much like an intervention. "Wait," she interrupted, faced her sister, "is Ennis saying I need a shrink?" She swiveled to the dining room which conveniently emptied out since their conversation began. Ennis probably carted Emily off to another room in expectation of an explosion.

"He never said that." Georgia backpedaled in an effort to rephrase, "Honey, he's concerned. That accident was traumatic enough but that added to the diagnosis, it's got to be overwhelming."

"It was. It is. I'll deal with it, okay? *Without* a shrink."

"You know I'm here if you want to talk," was the offer.

"And you know I'll call or come by if the pressure takes a toll." Or at least she should know it. Since childhood she only entrusted her secrets to her mother and Georgia. She was surprised Georgia dared mention a shrink. She hadn't spoken the work but the phrase "extra help" told Savannah plenty. Then she realized Ennis gently coerced her into it because her sister wasn't one to blatantly tempt fate. In case Georgia suffered an unexpected case of amnesia, Savannah reiterated, "I always come to you. You're both my shrink and priest." She leaned against the cabinet again, took another sip of tea. This time she sat the glass down with a gentler touch. "Ennis tell you I made a will?"

Georgia leaned against the sink next to her. "Yes," she replied softly. "While I'm in favor of being prepared, don't think for a minute this gives you permission to die."

A faint smile appeared, "Last I saw, I'm not in control of this ride. I get the Fast Forward and Stop buttons mixed up on our DVD player. With that degree of incompetence, I doubt God is gonna let me run my own show."

"I'm having a long heart to heart with Him later. Your job is to stay positive *and* keep me informed."

"Well, if I don't, I'm sure my dear husband will fill in the blanks."

Despite the seriousness, Georgia nearly smiled. Her thick Southern accent surfaced, "Are you trying to give the poor man a heart attack? By chance he finds out about your will then has to literally badger you into telling him about your biopsy. My God, Savannah, show the man some compassion. He deserves better."

She was right but no one would ever understand Savannah's reason for withholding the information. To keep peace, she agreed, "I'll try harder in the future. I told him, I'm not used to this marriage thing yet. It'll take some adjusting."

Georgia shook her head, sighed, "I imagine being married to you is like learning to ski in an avalanche. He's trying to survive it without too many scrapes."

10

Georgia cut a piece of Triple Chocolate Cake for Emily's trip home. Savannah noticed earlier that her sister displayed the dessert on Grandma Culberson's cake plate with pink tinted roses on the pedestal base. Georgia loved old heirlooms. Not that Savannah didn't. She treasured Grandma's china but because she leaned toward the clumsy side, she kept the set in an upper kitchen cabinet, away from her bumbling and fumbling fingers.

She watched her sister slice the bundt cake as her thoughts drifted back to the will. Georgia had no clue Grandma's china was bequeathed to her. Then it suddenly occurred to her: why not go ahead and give Georgia the dishes? She made a note to do that. The beautiful china was sitting around being appreciated from afar, not being used like Grandma wanted. Savannah knew she and Ennis would never use them, plus she was more "Chinet" than "china" anyway.

Georgia cut a large piece of cake for their guest – Savannah saw the secret wink she threw Emily's way. Georgia's "small" piece meant a slice two inches thick. *Now there's someone who'd make a great mom,* Savannah thought. Georgia had a natural kindness, a certain way with kids that made them flock to her. Savannah prayed Dane was the right man for her sister. He seemed to care deeply for her and treated Georgia very much like Ennis treated his new bride. Savannah hoped Emily was right about the wedding. Georgia deserved happiness – and she also deserved a passel of kids gathered around calling her "Mama".

Watching from nearby, Savannah noticed how much Georgia favored their mother. Her features and mannerisms reminded her of Charlene so much she found herself slipping back in time when the three of them gathered in the kitchen to prepare meals. As Georgia bantered with Emily, Savannah swore she witnessed a scene from long ago when Charlene laughed and joked with her daughters. The two chatting across the room appeared naturally comfortable together as if they'd known each other all their lives... The realization puzzled Savannah since Emily acted the same with her too. *There's something about that kid...*

Emily gifted Georgia with a smile that inspired a particular smile in response. A smile Savannah hadn't seen from her sister since her early twenties. One so subtle and particular, only Savannah or Seth might recognize it in Georgia's facial repertoire. It was a smile singularly reserved for their mother. Savannah saw it thousands of times when Charlene was alive. She figured the smile came naturally back then and if brought to Georgia's attention now, she'd deny its existence. The younger sister decided to keep quiet with the knowledge Georgia, in those few short hours, grew incredibly close to their new friend.

Emily turned to Savannah, her smile beaming. A peculiar calm washed over Savannah and an effortless grin surfaced in response. For a moment she heard and saw nothing except the girl across the way. And for some inexplicable reason she felt strangely familiar...

A touch on her shoulders drew her attention to Ennis who swept her hair aside and placed a soft kiss beneath her ear. "What are you thinking about?" he asked.

His arms slid around her waist and hugged her close. Savannah struggled to put her feelings into words. How did she phrase it without sounding ridiculous? She finally decided on, "Emily's different than other kids."

"You're tellin' me. Judging from her intelligence, her folks must be MENSA members."

"Yeah, but that's not what I mean. It's like we know each other."

"You do. You met tonight, remember?" he joked.

She leaned into him now, leisurely stroking the arms wrapped across her belly, "I can't explain it. Look at Georgia. She's so comfortable with Emily." She sighed. "Well, that was stupid to say, wasn't it? Georgia *always* looks comfortable with kids but she smiled a certain way that…" her voice trailed off.

Ennis leaned closer, whispering, "What way?"

"I'll sound insane."

"I'm used to that," he replied then chuckled at the gentle jab of her elbow. He kissed her cheek, "Tell me anyway."

"She only smiled like that with our mother."

Ennis answered her with a squeeze, as if he understood the distinction. Watching them another few moments, Ennis's warm breath caressed her ear, "You don't sound insane because I saw a different smile with you too. You only used it," he pointed toward the dining table, "with that little girl."

11

Savannah excused herself while the others chatted in the dining room. What a hell of a day, she bemoaned and once in the bathroom, she locked the door. She caught a glimpse of herself in the mirror and discovered why Emily hesitated to accept her dinner invitation. Savannah looked more akin to a strung out vagrant than a law enforcement officer. Of course the girl had no clue how monumentally awful the night had been. No one except herself and Ennis knew.

She ran the water until it warmed then washed her hands. She gave her nails a brief inspection. Was that blood embedded beneath the nails of her right hand? She'd washed numerous times at the station and when she arrived at Georgia's. How could there still be blood?

Savannah scrubbed her hands with soap and rinsed them. The faint discoloration faded but still remained visible to her. *Hayley's blood.* Savannah pulled every cabinet drawer open in search of a nail brush to clean with. When the cabinet stood empty of anything useful, she meticulously washed her hands again. *It's still there.* Hayley's painful screams shook her to the soul. As Savannah carried her, Hayley cried for her mother. The girl's face contorted with pain and fear and for the first time Savannah recalled a vague memory of damp warmth dripping down her arms. The warm sensation of blood.

Savannah turned the cold water on and splashed her face, hoping to rid herself of the memories. She closed her eyes only for the images to come alive again. The smells returned, the charred grass, the car engulfed in flames, the stench of burning flesh. Savannah retched into the sink and hurriedly splashed water on her cheeks. She held her cool hands to her throat in hopes of keeping supper down. *I killed Hayley. I've never killed a child in my life but I killed her.*

She patted her face dry with a nearby hand towel. She thought of Hayley's father. He lost his wife and daughter in a matter of minutes. By now, he'd been informed of the accident and by now he knew how drastically his life changed. Instead of setting out gifts beneath the tree, he was needed at the hospital for his baby son. Instead of celebrating Christmas, he needed to plan funerals. For him, the New Year meant loneliness and longing for what could have been. Lives shattered in an instant.

I killed Hayley. I shouldn't have moved her but I couldn't leave her either. Savannah's jaw and teeth ached from clenching so hard. *I've never killed a child – until tonight.* She lifted her vision to God to ask why. Why Hayley? And why did she and Ennis roll on scene first? Out of hundreds of cops, they arrived first, the chosen two to witness the accident's traumatic aftermath.

She pounded her fist on the cabinet. Why was that bastard out driving drunk? Drunk drivers didn't deserve to draw breath. She flinched at the statement. It hit too close to home. If God punished drunk drivers the way she wanted, she'd be right up front of the line. The one time she imbibed too heavily found her in a wrecked car too. Unlike the drunk that night, she hadn't mowed anyone down in the process of her stupidity. She gave God credit for protecting all the innocent people and letting her wreck herself out of wheels long enough to get sober. But who knew how many kids were saved Hayley's fate because of one angry drunken officer driving home one night?

Children shouldn't die. Not in wrecks and not because of drunks, pedophiles, murderers or accidents at the park. Like driving cars, cooking meals or having jobs, dying should be left to the adults.

Another look at her nails brought her frustration to an explosive level. The blood or whatever it was, still remained – a grim reminder of the night's hell. It *was* there, wasn't it? She wasn't imagining it, she couldn't be. She scrubbed her hands again. An assortment of memories haunted her while she washed. Hayley's twisted body, her bright flowered dress soaked with blood, Savannah's own bloodied blouse. The phone call. The diagnosis. The realization. *I have cancer.*

She dried her hands then jerked the bathroom door open. She headed straight for Georgia's bar and swiped the brandy. Beside it sat a snifter and shot glass. She opted for the shot glass. Just one tiny drink would help. One. And as for Georgia, Savannah just couldn't bring herself to care what she thought. She *needed* this drink.

Pouring the amber liquid into the glass, she sighed, feeling a tiny wave of relief mixed with guilt, the former overshadowing the latter. Anyone anxious to judge her actions could stand in her shoes a while. Now was not the time to scold or harangue. It was time to forget for one brief night.

Setting the bottle aside, she noticed a drop slid down the side of the glass. Her finger skimmed up the side, touched her tongue. The tiny taste persuaded her to lift the glass and tilt. The brandy flowed like silk past her tongue. Her sister only bought the best and when Savannah swallowed, the gentle warmth spread from her stomach in all directions. God bless paint thinner, she sighed.

A pang of shame tapped at her brain. She glanced up, "I'm sorry, Mama, but I need it tonight. Please understand. It's just tonight."

Standing in front of the mirror, Savannah stared at her left breast. From a casual glance, it looked as normal as any other woman's, at least with a blouse on. No one saw the needle mark from the biopsy or the little bruise it left. Cloaked by the rust colored pullover and beige suit jacket, her bosom passed for average and healthy.

She touched her breast, brushing her fingertips across the location of the biopsy. A wave of discomfort rolled through her chest, making her wince. Whatever happened to an ordinary existence? She wanted her life back. She longed to return to such menial tasks as paying the cable bill and the days she dreaded simple paperwork and not something as daunting as surgery or radiation – or worse. She yearned for the days when she and Ennis surrendered to their spontaneous desires. Once more guilt reared its head at the last thought. She'd refused him for days, using a variety of excuses until he finally stopped asking. Once more she became a poster child for making wrong decisions and hurting people she loved.

Savannah tilted the bottle again. The shot glass filled quickly with a splash over the side. She didn't clean it up right away. Instead she downed the brandy, praying it removed Ennis's hurt expression from her mind. Denying him anything positively killed her. Sure, he understood her actions *now* but during the week, she equated rebuffing him to ripping her heart out. "No more secrets, Ennis. I promise," she whispered in the silence. Then she tossed back a third swallow...

A soft rush of calm flowed in courtesy of the brandy. The familiar sensation relaxed her. Her hand instinctively reached for the bottle when a succession of four knocks on the door surprised her so bad she jumped. Strangely, her first thought was of Bobby and the infamous cold shower. It took only a second to realize the man banging on the door was Ennis. "You flush yourself down the toilet?" he asked.

Scooting the brandy to the corner of the cabinet and hopefully out of his sight, Savannah mopped up the spill then checked her reflection for any signs of tears. Before opening the door, she pasted on a smile and prayed it looked convincing. "Hey," she greeted, trying to nudge her way past. "Sorry 'bout that. My mind wandered while I tended to business."

Ennis blocked her way out. Forcing her vision to his, she prayed he didn't need to pee. The brandy sat in full view of the next occupant whether they merely washed their hands or had more pressing issues to deal with.

Thankfully, her husband didn't need to pee. No, he wanted a kiss which, in turn, struck a new terror inside her. He'd smell and taste the liquor on her breath then the questions would start in earnest. Before she shied away, Ennis framed her face between his large hands. His soft, warm lips pressed to hers that she knew felt firm and reluctant. The predictable response followed within the expected timeline – within two seconds.

Ennis pulled back, swept his tongue over his lips and frowned, "Where is it?"

She nodded behind her, "Ennis, don't be angry."

Ignoring the statement, he leaned over her shoulder, glanced around the corner. He spied the brandy on the cabinet and cursed under his breath. The look he leveled on her crushed her all over again. "How much did you drink?" he asked.

"Three," she answered truthfully. "I'm not drunk if that's what you're thinking."

"Believe me, that's not what I'm thinking." He reached past her, took the bottle and glass, "You don't need this."

Two times was enough to be clubbed with those particular words. "Don't," she literally bit her tongue to halt the heated warning. *Don't tell me what I need right now.* Before mentally regrouping a different reply, she heard her sister's voice coming down the hall. "Is she okay?" she was asking. Georgia rounded the corner to see Ennis holding the brandy and glass. "Oh, Savannah," she groaned, "you didn't."

Feeling ganged up on, she clenched her teeth, "Only three and I'm not a kid so don't lecture." She shouldered by Ennis and Georgia for some breathing room. On the way to the den, she overheard her sister tell Ennis, "Keep an eye on her. When she starts drinking –"

Savannah wheeled, "Don't you *even* mention twelve step programs to Ennis. I'm not like Daddy."

"I know. But when Mama got sick, you started drinking then too. I was telling Ennis to watch you, that's all."

The anger caused her to shake. Embarrassment from being caught darkened her face to the point it felt alive with heat. The mention of her past – a past that Ennis knew nothing about until now – swelled a rage inside her that only physical violence would cure. She hadn't kept it a secret, per se, she just never expected to sink to those abysmal depths again. Honestly, she never imagined wanting another drink so much. Now that she'd had a few, she craved more – just one more – but couldn't stomach disappointing her mother or Ennis.

Still in possession of the brandy, Ennis seized her arm like a father intent on punishing an unruly child. "'Scuse us," he said to Georgia and Emily.

"Ennis," Savannah warned, her vision fixed on his grasp. Her temper verged on exploding anyway and the fingers digging into her flesh served as the match lighting the fuse.

He hauled her up the stairway, his footfalls echoing in the room's silence. It briefly reminded her of her father's footsteps when he'd stomp up the stairs to beat the hell out of her. Anyone within hearing range knew he meant business.

Her husband's impatient gait caused the stairs to blur thanks to the few swallows of brandy she'd consumed. Maintaining a solid footing and not trip into the railing or fall down the stairs became a challenge of monumental proportions. Finally gaining a hold on the railing, Savannah glanced into the living room. Emily's rounded eyes followed the pair upstairs. Georgia, in contrast, assumed the stance of a fed-up parent with arms crossed and mouth pursed into a razor thin line.

The humiliating scene spurred Savannah's anger until she swore steam vented out her ears, "Ennis, you'd better let me go right now."

He said nothing in response, his grip on her arm remained taut. If Emily thought Ennis might hurt his wife, she'd have been mistaken, Savannah would have explained. But he stood a decent chance his wife might take a swing at *him* if he continued the rough treatment. If he graduated from the Rhett Butler School of Handling Women, he edged closer to having the behavior slapped out of him in much the same manner Scartlett smacked Rhett.

Brandy in hand, Ennis shoved the guest room door open then followed up by yanking her inside. He elbowed the door closed behind them. The instant he released her, she squared off with him, "What the hell are you doing hauling me up here like that? Why didn't you just grab my hair and drag me like a caveman would have?"

His hands planted on his hips, "I should have but there were children present."

Savannah bulled toward him only to be stopped short by his pointing finger, "Stay put," he commanded.

Way past spitting nails, she soared to spitting fire. Who was he to dictate to her? Is this what he thought marriage meant? To bully her, to control and order her around like a recruit at boot camp? Oh, he was *so* asking for it...

"It's me or this," Ennis lifted the brandy to her line of vision. "Choose."

The ultimatum temporarily derailed her rage. She stood poised to deliver a scathing dressing-down about respect or something to that effect. She couldn't actually remember now. Instead of lashing out, she settled on cranking out the meaning of his brief yet candid challenge. He wanted her to choose between drinking or him? *What*, she screamed to herself, *is wrong with him?* No one ever confronted her with such lunacy. No one dared to. Mentally faltering from his bold statement, a glimmer of rational thought peeked through. *Or no one cared that much until now.* Her expression evolved from pure anger to stunned confusion, "Are you nuts?"

"No. Choose."

"Okay, I choose you."

"Fine." With great ceremony, he placed the bottle on the nearby antique nightstand. "Then you won't need this anymore."

"What is your problem? I took three drinks in a glass," she indicated with her thumb and forefinger, "that tall. You can't get drunk on that." Using the same hand, she pointed accusingly, "I'm *not* an alcoholic, Ennis. I never have been."

He shook his head, his voice still calm, "Never said you were."

"That's how you and Georgia are treating me. You yourself know how hellacious this day – this week – has been." Emotion burst forth as tears, "I've got breast cancer. I never expected that. Not once." She said the words and for the first time, she actually heard how they sounded. *I've got breast cancer...* Through the tide of tears, she finished, "I've got the same disease that killed my mother and I can't cope. I'm not strong. She was strong, I'm not." She covered her face with her hands, "I'm falling apart and I haven't even had surgery yet. What if it's spread? What if it *isn't* small like Dr. Wyatt said?"

In that time, Ennis approached, put a gentle hand to her shoulder, "He's a doctor, he knows what he's doing."

Savannah backed away, her red, tear-streaked features darkened to a scowl, "Mama's doctor said hers was small too. Georgia and I insisted she get a second opinion and the cancer already spread so forgive me if doctors don't rate highly in my life."

"Savannah, listen to me. That was years ago. They've made huge strides in diagnosing and treating this."

Her blood pressure skyrocketed. The pulse pounding in her chest tapped inside her ears and into her fingertips and toes. She couldn't make him understand. She couldn't make him see what breast cancer did to her mother. She couldn't rip the awful memories from her own mind, much less describe them for someone who hadn't witnessed the evil of cancer.

Her brain screamed the fact Ennis tried to help, tried to reason with her. The alcohol overrode her brain and she stalked closer, "You didn't see what my mother went through. You weren't there, were you?"

Ennis stood his ground as she approached. He shook his head.

"I watched her die, Ennis. It wasn't quick and painless. She suffered and now I've got the same thing." She pointed to the offending breast, "Right here and I'm mostly to blame because I didn't do self exams like I should have."

"If it's small enough, you couldn't have felt it anyway."

"Don't," she ground through gnashed teeth, "make excuses for me. It's my fault I have this and now that I do, I can't cope without a little drink once in a while. Is that such a sin?"

"In your case, yes."

The alcohol, as usual, enhanced her worst trait and Savannah swung back to slap him. How dare him, she raged inside. Hayley didn't die in *his* arms. *He* didn't have breast cancer. *His* mother didn't suffer like hers did and for him to stand there and judge her – to dictate what was right and wrong...

Warm fingers clasped her wrist, stopping her intended assault. She winced as pain spiked up her arm to her shoulder. His hand met her wrist with enough force it felt like she hit a brick wall – or vice versa. Before she could react, Ennis brought her into his arms, hugged her against his chest.

Savannah struggled only briefly until melting into tears again. Ennis shushed her, "You can't drink because of your daddy and his problem. You've got me, Georgia, Seth and a lot of people for support." He emphasized with a squeeze and, "You don't need a drink, you need *us*."

The guilt of her actions blossomed into more tears. Ennis deserved better, Georgia was right. He deserved a stable wife without a vicious temper. At the very least, he deserved a wife who didn't try to slap his teeth out when he spoke the truth, "I'm sorry, Ennis. I'm sorry I tried to hit you." She wasn't fit for marriage, she told herself, but she loved him so much her heart ached. She held him tight, pleading, "Don't leave me. I won't do it again. Just don't leave me. I can't bear to lose you."

"Stop talkin' nonsense. I'm not going anywhere. All I ask is one favor."

She nodded, not trusting herself to say anything past apologizing for her deplorable behavior.

His embrace tightened, "Stop drinking. I've suspected for a while that's why you avoided liquor. I know you're not an alcoholic but drinking isn't good for you and we have enough to deal with right now."

"I'll stop." In her effort to forget the day's events, she also forgot how her temper mixed with drinking. She turned into R.J.'s Mini-Me upon the first swallow. If she continued drinking, she'd hurt Ennis emotionally and physically and once sober, she'd never be able to live with herself. "I'm sorry for trying to hit you –"

"Stop apologizing," he said. "Besides if you connected, I'd just take you home and put you over my knee." To drive his point home, he swatted her rear.

Savannah smiled a bit. He could *try* to put her over his knee, that much was true. But after remembering her husband's strength and determination, her smile waned. He'd do it if he wanted to.

A faint knock on the door interrupted her reply. Georgia peeked inside, "Sorry to intrude but Emily wanted a word with Savannah." She turned to her sister, "You up for it?"

Savannah wiped tears away and nodded. What could the girl want with her? She glanced at her watch. The bus wasn't leaving for another thirty minutes so getting back to the station wasn't imminent. She heard Georgia speaking softly to the child, telling her to go on inside.

Ennis touched Savannah's cheek, "I'll be right outside. We'll talk later."

She merely nodded an agreement. Her husband and sister meant well. Drinking led to worse problems, yes, but sometimes a soul needed fortification to cope with devastating news. Some women, she assumed, coped decently well with it. Her mother's battle with breast cancer geared her toward the morbid side where she equated breast cancer to a death sentence.   Some news shouldn't be approached in a sober condition, much less *dealt with* in one but she had no choice.

Emily stepped in and closed the door.   "Your situation is different," the girl began.

"What situation?" Savannah asked, confused. If Emily joined the choir about drinking, containing her anger would prove mighty difficult.

"Your health situation. It's different than your mother's. You have the advantage of early detection, specialists, modern treatments, and you're aware of your family history. She didn't have any of that."

"How do you know?" She didn't bother concealing her cynicism. The little girl headed to Memphis for Christmas never met Charlene Prince. As she chattered about people she didn't know, Savannah bit her tongue against lashing out. She reminded herself the little girl had yet to experience the dark side of life, the general disappointments, the cruelty of the world, and the deaths of people she loved. Wise as the child sounded, she was still just a child.

However, in those few brief seconds, Savannah detected a transformation in the girl. Emily's mannerisms evolved and matured. She moved toward Savannah who developed a sudden urge to step back.

As if sensing it, Emily stopped, the corners of her mouth lifted slightly, "Do you believe in angels?"

The question caught her off guard. Angels? She believed people used the word until it ran on rims, sure. But real angels? "I never thought about it. Why?"

The girl clasped Savannah's hand and tugged her to her knees until they faced each other. Emily continued, "Do you believe your mother is watching over you?"

In some ways, yes, especially when life threatened to overwhelm her. She swore Charlene's spirit embraced her as she had when Savannah was a child. Today's news more than overwhelmed her. It promised to drown her. "Yes, I do believe she watches over me."

On any other day, Savannah would have felt stupid conversing with a child about her mother's spirit. She should have been committed, she knew that, because this child's presence didn't feel childlike. Emily exhibited a very adult presence, one with a genuine wisdom. Most of all, the presence seemed familiar to Savannah.

Emily's small hand touched Savannah's cheek, "She tries to guide and protect you. She wants to help you, like God wants to. You have to trust God through these difficult times. You've always been independent and strong but God is stronger. Let Him help."

Looking into the little girl's eyes, Savannah sensed an affection that touched her soul. The pretty green pools held an intimacy that she'd not seen in many years. In her heart, she realized she no longer spoke to a child, "I'm trying to let God help but I really want Mama," Savannah felt her composure crumbling. "I need her to hold me and say it'll be alright. I want her with me."

Emily opened her arms and hugged her, "She's with you. She'll always be with you."

One step away from Rose Austin Psychiatric Hospital. That was Savannah. If she told Ennis or Georgia about her conversation with Emily, they'd pack her suitcase and drop her off for evaluation. Either that or enroll her in rehab. She wasn't drunk, she assured herself. At her worst she never hallucinated when she drank. She'd heard her mother's voice all evening and felt her presence. She wasn't tipsy or crazy. The relief flowing through her while she and Emily embraced – that was *real*.

In the following few minutes, they began preparing Emily for her next bus. Savannah still didn't feel right sending a child alone on such a long trip. She couldn't bear to think what might have happened to Emily if she hadn't driven past the terminal when she did.

While the others gathered food for Emily's late night snack, Savannah padded to the living room to let her supper and the day's news digest. She passed by the brandy and noticed the pointed look her sister aimed her way. Savannah held her hands up in surrender, a silent promise to keep her hands off.

She meandered between the couch and coffee table to Georgia's writing desk. She plunked down in the leather chair. The brand new Dell desktop computer already showed Georgia's personality with its screensaver of family photos. Leaning back, Savannah watched each photo fade in, and like a memory, hold briefly then fade away. The first picture, one of all three siblings as kids, reminded her of the time. It was Seth's birthday. He had an arm around each sister, his strong jaw lifted, his grin infectious. It faded to another picture, this one of R.J. and Charlene as newlyweds. Savannah committed the sight to memory. Their mother truly looked happy and surprisingly R.J. appeared sober. The two presented quite an attractive couple at the time. The pixels began to vanish, giving way to a photo of Georgia and Dane together. Watching the screen felt akin to flipping through a photo album. Savannah's picture was next, then one of Seth and his family. Lindsey, then Dylan followed. After that was a photo taken at a cousin's wedding of Savannah and Ennis together. The next picture brought tears to her eyes. Hers and Ennis's wedding portrait. His mouth curved into a proud smile, hers into a joyful one. Savannah also recognized something else in her expression: contentment. She never imagined marriage could provide a solid feeling of security and satisfaction. They still acted like newlyweds, even with their occasional spats. The argument that night, thankfully, was a rare occurrence and like that night, the other fights ended in an embrace, a few tears but always an apology.

The computer's steady hum dominated the quiet room while gifting her with images from her past. Beside the machine sat a notebook of handwritten notes. If a person's handwriting described their personality, Georgia's fit her perfectly. Neat, stylish and just enough flair to impress. Savannah, on the other hand, would be labeled a serial killer. Not even upgrading to computers for filling out paperwork helped her scrawl. She really needed to tidy up her scribble. Maybe after surgery she'd dedicate the time.

Savannah perused Georgia's notes for her next book. Her sister's talent amazed her. She wondered how Georgia created the stories she did. Looking at a handwritten outline, she noticed it was like a recipe. A little of this, a dash of that, and a liberal sprinkle of something else. She was proud of Georgia's success. People from all over knew her by sight and by name. Writing not only served as a career but a release. After Matthew served divorce papers, Georgia's writing dried to a trickle, leaving not only divorce lawyers hounding her but her agent and publishing house too. Then along came Dane, rascal that he was. He was a good man and Savannah didn't resent him visiting her sister. Turned out he made Georgia smile and laugh more in a few weeks than Savannah saw in months. When the pages began to flow again and the computer keyboard produced the customary rhythm, Savannah knew Dane Rutherford was good medicine.

A few more photos drifted on and off the screen until one appeared of Savannah in her uniform. The picture, taken only two years earlier, showed her pride in wearing the dress blue uniform, the gold shield gleaming. Her commendations numbered an even six, lined up perfectly in a row beneath the badge. Earlier that evening, retiring from the job seemed easy, even the right thing to do. All cops burned out at some point or to some extent. Staring at the photo as it faded into electronic oblivion reinforced the old feeling that leaving the job required more thought. The passion for justice still held strong. She wanted to make a difference in someone's life because of that badge but the uncertainty of illness arrived, forcing her to analyze more of her life than the job.

Savannah recalled the day she mentioned her career plans to her parents. Understandably both received the news with a silence that made her uneasy. "Are you sure about this?" Charlene had inquired, her inflection revealing her shock.

When Savannah nodded, R.J. took his turn in a less than subtle way, "It's that damn Bobby, ain't it? He talked up being a deputy and you're just gullible enough to believe him."

She managed to retain her composure, even when Charlene gently scolded R.J.. Her mother, bless her heart, always assumed the role of go-between. Without taking sides, she rationalized, "Honey, law enforcement is a tough job, not only physically but emotionally. I'm sure Bobby explained that. You'll see things no one should."

"Especially a woman," R.J. stomped to the phone. "Women shouldn't be cops. I'm calling that bastard and tellin' him to stay away from you."

"Daddy, please stop," Savannah pleaded. "Bobby didn't convince me. It was my choice."

He pointed the receiver like a giant finger, "Don't lie to me. You been spendin' your weekends with him. He's responsible for this."

"I went on ride-alongs with him but he didn't twist my arm."

"You oughta be helpin' manage those orchards instead of carrying guns. Those orchards are your future, they're the Prince legacy."

"Daddy, too many cousins manage them already. It wouldn't do me any good to get involved."

"You can pick peaches, can't ya? If you're too dumb for anything else, pick fruit."

"R.J., stop," Charlene admonished. "She's obviously thought about this and wants a career in law enforcement. Support her decision."

"Like hell I will."

Savannah emerged from the memory, glad for its demise. R.J. never supported his children, not like Charlene did. Not on decisions about school sports, and more importantly, their career choices.

The thought virtually melted away as another picture appeared on the computer screen. Emily's picture. The young girl smiled in a way Savannah recognized as a genuine joyful smile. Since arriving at the house, Emily gifted her and Georgia with the same smile.

As the picture faded, Savannah closed her eyes then shook her head to force her overburdened mind back to reality. Emily's picture shouldn't have been on Georgia's computer and Savannah now wondered if she saw it at all. No, she definitely saw it and if her sister argued otherwise, she'd show her the photo. The surreal night continued playing tricks on her no matter which way she turned. *Damn*, she lamented, *drinking doesn't even help anymore.* She rose from the chair only for her vision to lock on another picture – one Georgia never displayed until now – one that confirmed Savannah's point or her insanity. On the writing desk sat a five by seven frame. In that frame was yet another picture of Emily. Slowly Savannah reached for the picture. Once in hand, she examined it closely. The black and white picture revealed a girl with the same dark wavy hair, the same features and, looking closer, the same thin scar running along the outside of her right hand. This was Emily.

Before bringing it to Georgia's attention only to have her deny the discovery, Savannah opened the back of the frame. Georgia was a nut for labeling everything so the photo was sure to have a name and date.

The back slid off easily and the sight before her made Savannah literally lose her breath. The words written clearly in Georgia's flair read, "Charlene Culberson, age 5."

"Georgia," she heard herself call weakly. Her voice lacked the determination she'd planned so carefully to employ. Instead, she sounded on the verge of tears. Then she recalled Georgia's blanched features upon seeing the child. *She knew...* She knew immediately Emily looked like their mother and hadn't said a word.

Savannah called her sister again, this time while drawing nearer to the brandy again. "Georgia," she added more determination – it was either that or panic – to the summons.   She tilted the brandy into a snifter. The first time she drank the stuff she labeled it paint thinner as her sister reminded. Even paint thinner had its attributes, Savannah reflected, especially when the person stood on the very precipice of lunacy.

But when she cradled the snifter in her palm, she hesitated. Lifting it to her lips essentially became a battle between pain and common sense. R.J.'s answer to life sat in her hand, waiting, taunting her to partake, to get hooked like he was. When she drank, Savannah became no better than her father at his pickled best. Depending on the liquor, she became so angry that she toed a thin line that easily escalated to violence. That's when the realization dawned that the darkness of Robert Jefferson Prince lurked deep inside her, waiting to emerge, to hurt people emotionally and physically. Unlike her father, she'd thankfully avoided hitting people but managed to bung up her fist a couple of times on innocent walls and cars.

The fierce scowl her sister laid on her earlier reared its head, giving Savannah pause before throwing back a swallow. *Oh hell,* she griped. Sisters could be such a pain in the ass. She sat the snifter down with a sigh.

"Good move," a voice said from behind. It was Georgia. At least she was proud of the decision instead of breathing fire at her like before. Savannah turned to face her with a lethal expression, "Why didn't you tell me she looked like Mama? God sakes, I nearly had a stroke when I saw that picture on your desk."

Georgia's expression went through a plethora of emotion in mere milliseconds. Surprise, dismay, confusion then finally a hint of sadness, "I thought you'd seen pictures of her as a child."

"Yeah," was the deadpan, "that's why I stood there with a stupid grin on my face when I introduced you."

"Well, I didn't know you hadn't..." she stepped around Savannah to pour the brandy back, stopped then took a healthy swallow herself. "I mean, you've got pictures of her."

"As a full-fledged, twenty-something year-old woman. Not as a five year-old."

Georgia threw down another swallow much to her sister's jealousy. With narrowed vision Savannah removed the snifter from her sister possession, "Unless you're sharing, do you mind not flaunting the fact you can drink that stuff without people labeling you a lush?"

"You're not a lush. You just have a tendency to act like Daddy when you drink."

Savannah shot an incredulous frown her way, "Well, *that* makes me feel much better, thank you. Instead of a lush, I'm a hateful, abusive jerk."

"Only when you drink."

The younger sister took the comment to heart causing Georgia to smile, "I'm joking, Savannah. Try to smile. You're prettier when you do."

12

Emily sat between Ennis and Savannah as he drove to the bus station. For Savannah, a feeling of contentment crept in during the ride. Having a child sandwiched safely between them felt fulfilling, like she found the missing piece of their puzzle. When Emily's head leaned against Savannah's shoulder and she took her hand, the detective's aspiration momentarily shifted from the job to becoming a mother. She'd have another talk with Ennis later, after the surgery and subsequent treatment.

A bolt of fear ran through her. What if she couldn't have kids after the treatment? What if radiation rendered a woman infertile? She'd heard chemotherapy could and prayed that particular treatment wouldn't be necessary. What if she'd lost the only opportunity to have a sweet little girl like Emily or Lindsey or even an adorable son like Dylan?

Emily's fingers tightened around Savannah's hand, "It'll be okay."

"I hope you're right," was all she brought herself to say. Determined to change the subject, she reached in her jacket, handed the girl her card, "Take this and if you have any problems, call me, alright? I'll find a way to get you help, I promise."

Emily studied the card in the muted light of passing streetlamps. Savannah pointed to a number, "That's my cell phone and I wrote my home number on the back. Call any time, even if you just want to talk."

"We're here," Ennis pulled the Dodge Ram into the parking lot and cut the engine. A bus idled nearby with the doors open to allow passengers to board.

Savannah took note of the time. They had only minutes to spare. She turned in the seat and gathered Emily's coat to zip it, "Put your mittens on and don't forget your hat. It's cold out there and you don't want to get sick."

"She's only going from the truck to the bus," Ennis hinted.

"She can take them off once she's inside the bus," she informed then zipped the coat. "The weather's freezing. I nearly got chilled coming out of the house. Where's your hat, sweetheart?"

Obviously delighted with the attention, Emily grinned, reached in her coat pocket and plopped the stocking cap on her head.

Ennis watched, seemingly impressed with the thorough wrapping Savannah gave the girl. His wife's vision strayed momentarily to him. She winked as a gentle smile curved his lips.

"Mittens?" the detective inquired then watched the girl reach in the other pocket to retrieve the lilac mittens to match her stocking cap. Emily slipped them on as Savannah leaned to the floorboard for the Barbie suitcase. When she straightened in the seat, two small arms encircled her neck, "I had a great time," Emily said. "Thank you."

Savannah returned the embrace, "Anytime, sweetie. Call when you're in town again and Ennis, Georgia and I would love to see you."

The girl refused to let go, "You would make a great mom."

The statement initially caught Savannah off-guard but she recovered quickly with a thank you and, "Maybe someday, after my surgery, Ennis and I will discuss a family."

Emily pulled away, her small mitten covered hands framed Savannah's face, "You can't always be a policewoman but you can always be a mom."

The bus terminal door swung open and people stepped outside only to wither from the bitter breeze. The ones wearing coats pulled them tighter around their bodies or cowered from the cold. Snow began falling again in the short span of time they sat in the truck. Large, fat flakes drifted onto the windshield and in no time, a thin blanket covered it and the Dodge's windshield. The sudden flurry of snowfall surprised Ennis, "You're right. Emily needed to bundle up."

Still captive between two lilac clad hands, Savannah shivered when Ennis opened the driver door and a cold gust rolled through the once cozy cab. Emily held eye contact as she emphasized, "Remember that, Savannah. You can always be a mom and both you and Georgia will make wonderful mothers."

Savannah nodded, sensing the words came from someone else, not the young girl with her. The dome light blinked off as Ennis closed the door and rounded the passenger side. In the soft illumination of the terminal lights, she felt a connection – yet again – to the eyes staring back at her, to the voice speaking to her.

"I'll remember," she replied.

Ennis knocked on the passenger door. Emily gave Savannah another hug then they braced for the impending chill as Ennis opened the door. He offered his hand to his wife, helped her down then reached in for Emily who held to him like his own. Once her feet hit the ground, she took Savannah's hand in hers as Ennis trailed behind with the Barbie suitcase and brown bag full of food Georgia sent along. The older sister packed an abundance of goodies – enough that Savannah felt confident there was plenty for all the passengers if hunger set in. Once Emily reached her destination, she'd have enough to feed both herself and father which, Savannah supposed, was Georgia's main objective.

"Emily, it was a pleasure to meet you," Ennis said. "I hope we see each other again."

"We will," the girl replied confidently. "And thank you both for a wonderful evening."

"Thank you for joining us," Savannah said. "You're welcome back anytime." She took the suitcase and food from him and escorted Emily onto the bus. "Let's find you a place to sit." Glancing around the crowd, she noticed most of the travelers showed their weariness from a long bus ride. Savannah labeled a few unsavory, weary or not. She wasn't allowing the little girl anywhere near them. Instead, she searched for a female, preferably older.

Scanning the passengers with empty seats beside them, her vision ultimately settled on an elderly woman, her gray hair pulled back in a bun. Upon sight of the young girl, her heavily lined features beamed with what Savannah considered hope the child might sit with her. She pointed to the older woman, "How 'bout next to that lady in blue?"

Emily surveyed the smiling woman, her frail hands now moving her purse to her lap and patting the seat beside her. She nodded and hugged Savannah once more, whispering, "God rewards those with good hearts. You have a good heart, Savannah. I've known that all along. Stay strong and trust Him."

There it was again. That feeling she couldn't explain but

cherished while it lasted. The comforting warmth lingered as they embraced. Savannah told Emily she'd try harder to trust God. She was still enrolled in the baby step class of doing so but she promised. Savannah reminded, "Don't forget. Call me when you get to your daddy's."

"Okay," Emily said again. "I'm glad I met you. I'm glad I met you all."

"Me too, sweetie. You take care now." She rose to her feet and addressed the bus driver, "How many stops between here and Memphis?"

The burly driver, looking more than exhausted, managed a smile as he answered.

"And you'll be driving the whole way?" she asked.

He nodded in a less than enthusiastic manner. Savannah stepped closer, spoke in a near whisper, "She's traveling alone. Would you mind keeping an eye on her until you get to Memphis? Her father's supposed to pick her up."

"I'll watch her."

"Thanks, I appreciate it." Savannah reached in her jacket and handed him a card, "This is my cell number. If anything happens or no one comes for her, let me know, okay?" The driver already began to nod when she rephrased, "Could you just call me either way? Just want to make sure she's safe."

He angled the card toward the light to see the Atlanta Police Department insignia and her name, "No problem, Detective. It's my last stop for the night so I'll hang around for her ride."

Upon arriving home, Savannah fielded calls from Seth, his wife Leah and one from Dane. Her brother stumbled for words, giving her the impression he pieced together his intended speech and once hearing her voice, the speech evaporated. After a goodly amount of tripping over his tongue, Seth settled on, "I love you, sis, and I'm here for you."

Leah, on the other hand, jabbered a marathon to Savannah about the strides made in breast cancer treatments. Facts and figures blazed across the phone lines so fast, Savannah barely kept up with them. Because Seth's wife was a nurse, she found a way to ease so many of the worries burdening Savannah. So also broached a touchy subject, "I know your mother had breast cancer but that was several years ago. Back then they treated it much differently. A lot of times they removed the breast, lymph nodes and muscle." Leah went on to explain – like Dr. Wyatt had in limited terms that night – that radiation would probably be the best treatment if the tumor was small.

Leah mentioned another important matter weighing down Savannah's mind and spirit. "I know you're worried about Ennis."

With Ennis in the shower, Savannah felt free to be honest, "I am worried. The treatments will drain my energy so I probably won't feel good until they're finished." When she hesitated, Leah evidently sensed the impending concern and allowed her time to gather her courage. Savannah took an unsteady breath, "And I'll have scars from the surgery..."

"Savannah," her sister-in-law's voice softened, "he didn't marry you for your breasts."

The phrasing brought a tiny smile then a chuckle. When Leah

spelled it out that way, it made perfect sense. It wouldn't relieve the entirety of her distress but it helped. She wiped a tear, "I suppose he didn't."

"Of course not. He's a sweet man and he loves you. Not just your legs or your nose or your breasts, he loves you as a whole, for your outer *and* inner beauty."

Savannah remembered when she went to meet Ennis's family in Texas. One night when she and Ennis were alone he caught sight of her father's handiwork. Scars striped her lower back where, in her younger years, R.J. whipped her so hard she missed school for three days. Savannah remembered Ennis's whisper touch across her flesh, his anger building as he traced the scars. He wanted to kill R.J. for abusing his daughter. Despite his anger, Ennis made her feel beautiful that night and if she hadn't been already madly in love with Ennis Rutherford, she'd have fallen hard that instant.

So yes, Ennis loved her entirely, head to toe, inside and out, temper and all. The poor guy, Savannah thought. He had no idea what madness he married into until now.

The conversation with Leah lifted her spirits more than the one she'd had with Georgia which surprised her. Of course, the one with her sister was laced with cautions not to drink. Leah never mentioned the brandy – and Savannah would bet her life Georgia told her and Seth everything. To her credit, Leah stayed on topic without lecturing.

Dane's call equaled Seth's in that he struggled to find words that comforted without offending or causing more grief. Savannah found herself comforting *him* rather than the other way around.

"I'm comin' out for your surgery," he'd said. "In fact, I'll hop a plane tomorrow."

"Dane, I'll be fine. Stay with your family for now and I'll call about the surgery."

He paused for the longest until asking, "It's small, right? The... the thing is small."

"Yes, the doctor assured me the tumor is small and hopefully he'll just take it and some lymph nodes. We'll have to wait for the results to see if it's spread."

As though she'd given him food for thought, his voice lost its awkwardness, "If it's small, chances are it hasn't spread, Peach. There's a real good chance."

"That's what I keep hearing." She tried to sound confident while attempting to assure Dane it was a simple process and nothing to worry about. By the end of their conversation he hadn't sounded any more convinced than she felt but he was more upbeat than when he called.

By the time she finished updating everyone who called then changed into her pajamas, slumber conveniently evaded her. Normally she could tell if Ennis fell asleep by his guttural snores. That night the room fell so quiet the silence irritated her.

Savannah slowly pushed the covers back, sat up on the bedside and buttoned the top button of her sleepy sheep flannel top. The sky blue pajamas sported dozens of cartoon sheep jumping over fences and beds. Ennis always teased her about the pajamas saying she looked twelve years old in them but after years of wear, they became her most comfortable winter attire. She'd wear them to threads because she was convinced pitching them out was a sin somewhere in the universe.

She rubbed her eyes then looked around the dark room. The clock on the bedside table read 3:26 in the morning. After little debate, she decided to busy her mind and read instead of reviewing the hellacious day again. Trying to stand without waking Ennis, she rose to her feet and waited for signs she disturbed him. She wished he'd start snoring. The concept of snoring indicated normalcy, the one thing she yearned for.

She dared take a step toward the living room. He didn't awaken. Another step. Nothing. One more step. "Where are you going?" he asked, not a trace of sleep in his voice.

She sighed, "I can't sleep so I was gonna read, maybe fix some warm milk or something."

Ennis threw the covers back and levered to his feet, "Well, let's do it together. Between the two of us we can stumble on something to help us sleep. Tomorrow's a big day. Lindsey and Dylan are expecting us to check out their loot from Santa."

Savannah's vision roamed her husband's muscular physique. His bare chest sprinkled liberally with dark curls and hard muscle tapered to lean, strong hips currently wearing navy blue pajama bottoms. He defined sexy whether naked or fully clothed. Soon, she prayed, they could resume their frisky nature. The trials and tribulations of the past week took a toll on her. At the earliest opportunity, she planned to jump him – if he didn't get to her first. "At this rate," she said, "I'm not gonna look anymore awake than Seth or Leah." She waited for him to throw on a robe then they meandered into the living room.

She flipped on the light, "I still haven't heard from Emily or the bus driver. I hope nothing happened."

Ennis peeled off to the kitchen. The light from the fridge illuminated the small room until he switched on the light. Savannah heard the clank of a pan on the stove and assumed he took her literally. He was warming milk for them.

"Stop worrying," he called from the kitchen. "You'd worry for everyone if you could."

"The bus probably arrived an hour ago. Thirty minutes ago at the least." Giving the clock a disparaging scowl, she wondered aloud, "Should I call the state patrol?"

"Savannah, she's fine. The driver probably forgot and chances are she did too. Once she saw her daddy, we were the last people on her mind. You know how kids are."

She plopped on the couch with a long sigh, watched the goldfish swim lazily in their bowl. "Just wish I could hear something, that's all."

After a few minutes, he rounded the corner of the kitchen armed with two mugs of warm milk. Handing one off to her, he sat beside her then chuckled at her attire, "You still look like a kid in those things."

Savannah took a tentative sip of milk. How he did it she'd never know. "This is perfect. Why don't you open a coffee shop?"

He nudged her with an elbow, "You willin' to be my waitress?"

Holding the mug in both hands, she smiled, "I could be persuaded."

The sound of her phone startled her so badly, she nearly dropped the heavy mug in her lap. Ennis helped her steady it then fetched the ringing phone. Savannah clicked on to hear a male voice, "This Detective Prince?"

"Yes, it is."

"This is Cecil Landis, the bus driver from this evening."

"Yes, Cecil. Thank you for calling. Did Emily make it okay?"

There was a hesitation that forced Savannah to abandon the milk to the side table. *This isn't good news*, her gut said. *So prepare yourself...*

Ennis sensed something wrong and leaned in to listen as Cecil continued, "I've spent an hour trying to figure a way to tell you this."

Memories of Hayley flashed in her mind, feeding the bitter sickness rising in her stomach. Not another little girl. Not *Emily...* Her voice laced with alarm, "What happened to Emily?"

"That's just it. We was pullin' into a stop and some folks got off but I made sure she was still on board. When we started up again, she came to me, handed me a note. I swear, Detective, I watched that little girl like she was mine. But when I looked back up, she was gone. Completely gone."

Her tone adopted the massive panic rolling through her brain. Ennis put a hand to her knee in an attempt to calm her. It didn't work, "Gone? I don't understand –"

"Neither do I. We was drivin' a good fifty miles an hour. One second she's there, the next she's gone. I looked in my rearview mirror and even the old lady she was with freaked out."

Savannah wasn't sure the brandy cleared her system yet. Initially, she thought someone kidnapped Emily but the driver stressed the girl was on the bus at all times – but she, what, disappeared during the trip to Memphis?

The bourbon beckoned to her. It began as a whisper and grew in volume forcing Savannah to fight it off. It didn't promise to straighten out the convoluted situation she faced but it promised to ease her mind for a while. And judging by his expression, Ennis might have joined her in imbibing.

She recalled something the driver said which temporarily expelled thoughts of drinking, "You mentioned a note. What did it say?"

The reference only intensified Cecil's confusion, "Oh, yeah. The note." Savannah heard paper crinkling in the background as he unfolded the note. Waiting for him to read it rated up there with the surreal activities of the day. Hayley's death, the diagnosis, the weird visit from Emily... Savannah prayed her world made sense the next day.

"And that's a strange thing too." Cecil cleared his throat then enunciated carefully, "It's addressed to you and reads as such. 'I am with you always. I love you, Little Flower.' That's what it says, I swear. Does it mean anything to you?"

She guessed it was a spontaneous reaction to the name. She further attributed it to the connection she felt with the girl. A connection that completely defied logic. Tears welled fast and furious in her eyes. They fell too quickly to catch or stop them.

Witnessing her sudden flood, Ennis stared in disbelief then handed her a box of tissues from the nearby side table.

Savannah felt sure her husband questioned her sanity again but the nickname her mother gave her as a child brought an unexpected wave of emotion to the forefront. Snuffling back the tears, she scarcely regrouped her composure to answer Cecil, "Actually, it means a lot."

After the conversation ended, Ennis moved the phone to the table, his tone hesitant, his features more than cautious, "Are you okay?"

She wiped a stray tear, blew her nose, "I will be now."

He treaded lightly into the subject, "That note affected you pretty fierce."

A tremulous smile crossed her lips. Her eyes welled again at the remembrance of the night's events but she managed to curb them, "It's a personal thing. I don't know that you'd understand because I can hardly believe it myself."

"I know what I heard. That kid called you her flower. You knew her all of what, two, three hours? That's kinda chummy for a short visit."

Taking a chance, Savannah explained, "My mother called me Flower when I was little. There was a field close to my school and when I'd find flowers, I'd bring them to her so she called me her flower."

"Your *mother*?" the silence that ensued said her husband teetered on the verge of either hitting the bottle himself or calling the mental ward to cart her off. "But that's impossible," he continued. "How could that kid know what your mother called you?"

As unbelievable as it sounded, Savannah understood precisely how the girl knew. The little girl who looked like Charlene at that age, the sound of her voice, the recognition in her eyes... It all came together to mean one thing. Earlier that day Savannah asked for a miracle. Emily may have appeared to be a normal five year-old to Ennis but looking back on the evening's events, even Georgia sensed something different about the girl. She saw it upon *sight* of her.

A gentle smile curved Savannah's lips. Whether she verbalized the fact or not, Savannah knew who Emily was and thanked God for sending her.

13

There were two surefire ways to get a phone to ring, Savannah decided. One, win the lottery. Two, be diagnosed with a potentially terminal illness. Besides the usual calls from Georgia, Seth, Leah, Dane and Mama, she answered calls from a few cousins on the Prince side.

Later, the cousins from the Culberson side wormed their way out of the woodwork. These people – Savannah used the term loosely – called for basically one reason relating to number two, the potential terminal illness. Savannah calculated the time it took for the news to circulate through the entire Prince and Culberson families. One day, twelve hours and fifteen minutes. Telephone, telegraph and Tell-A-Culberson, the gossip mongers of North Georgia. If it was news, a Culberson knew it, and courtesy of Linda, Teresa or Abby, it got mangled into half-truths and embellishments along the way. The trio's talent for creating something out of nothing was renowned throughout the Prince side of the family. There were times when Savannah wondered if the Culbersons drove R.J. to his alcoholic state. Drunk probably sounded better than dealing with them stone cold sober. On that note, Savannah sympathized with him.

Past the strained niceties, Linda's clipped Georgia brogue

proceeded, "Honey, you just tell us what you need and it's yours. I know the devastation breast cancer can inflict upon a person. You remember Teresa had it and they nearly took her breast. I told her they should have taken both, you know, to stave off future problems. And those chemo treatments were harder than Aunt Emma's fruitcake. Honey, I hope you don't have those. My Lord, what she went through..."

As Linda described in great detail about her sister's battle with the treatments, Savannah concentrated on Ennis who relaxed at the dining table with the morning's Journal-Constitution. His six-foot frame looked striking in the blue plaid lounging pants and navy blue robe gathered around his bare chest. Wisps of dark hair curled into view above the robe's tie, giving her a perfect view for weathering the current storm on the phone. She loved watching him, his muscular form moving with ease and fluidity no matter what he did. He made something as simple as reaching for his coffee look refined.

"...thought the girl was history but she pulled through unlike your poor mama. I remember how Aunt Charlene suffered," Linda continued. "Felt so bad when she passed on."

The last few sentences drew Savannah from her brief fantasy and scalded the last of her patience. "Not as bad as I felt," she snapped. "She was my mother."

Ennis glanced up from the morning paper. His vigilant effort to divert her attention from Charlene's situation succeeded to a point but by the set of his mouth, he saw it going down in flames. His brow dove between his eyes, "Who the hell is that?"

She waved the question off. Linda and her sister never missed an opportunity to remind people of their painful losses then backtrack as though the "faux pas" wasn't intended.

As expected, Linda agreed a bit too emphatically, "Of course, honey, of course. But considering what happened, have you prepared for the worst, just in case? Y'know, write a will and everything? You've got those orchards and the money your grandpa left you. A person can't be too careful these days, what with the government's greediness."

It always amazed her how the majority of the Culberson cousins found time to nose into another's affairs. The orchards and money were on the Prince side of the family anyway. Savannah had a suspicion that the Culberson Trio had their sights set on any monetary gains her death might leave behind. Teresa, Abby and Linda circled like vultures when they smelled the possibility of death. Linda's phone call merely reaffirmed her purpose for making the will. To prevent leeches from attaching to what they "thought" was rightfully theirs.

"Don't forget our family's greediness, Linda. Their sticky fingers put the Feds to shame," Savannah saw Ennis peer over the paper again the basically wad it between his fists. She tried to smile albeit tensely, "Yes, I have a will and I do not intend for my family to have to use it."

"Savannah," Ennis called in a tone that refused argument. "I need to make a call. *Right now.*"

"My heavens," Linda feigned astonishment, "what a bossy man. Sounds just like your daddy. I never expected *you* to tolerate that sort of behavior."

"Ennis is nothing like Daddy and to answer your question, it's actually nice to have someone look after me like he does. I gotta go. Thanks for calling and no, none of the Culbersons inherit from me. Bye-

bye now." She resisted the urge to slam the phone down. After all, if she did, it couldn't ring with another long lost cousin fifteen times removed. God, she hated the fact she shared the news with a soul. Only Ennis needed to know but once Georgia knew, that was the beginning of the end.

She headed Ennis off before he asked, "It's part of my mother's family. You've never met them and hopefully you never will. Grace is the only decent one and she's smart enough to keep a low profile."

"This Linda, she asked you about a will?" Ennis's anger percolated beneath the surface. His jaw muscles clenched, his hands fisted. The remnants of the morning paper now lay crumpled into an unsalvageable mess on the dining table. She nodded slightly, "That term 'having a screw loose' only applies if you have screws to begin with."

"Why haven't I met these people?"

"Because," she replied truthfully, "you wouldn't have married me if you had met them."

The phone rang once more, prompting Ennis to march directly to it and answer. Savannah pitied the caller. Her husband's tone left no doubt as to his mood. Then to her surprise, Ennis changed to a happier disposition, "It's Bobby."

Before stopping herself, she winced. Her ear hurt in concert with her brain and her tongue was too tired to even pant its weariness. She entertained the whimsy of checking into the hospital under an assumed name, just to get peace from the damn phone. She took the receiver and prepared herself for yet another long discussion.

Bobby wasted no time past the greetings and formalities, "Have you had a second opinion?"

Bless his heart, Bobby treated her like a sister. "Well, my M.D. found the spot on the mammogram and recommended Dr. Wyatt who also did an ultrasound and a biopsy, the latter of which I don't recommend to the fainthearted." In truth, her physician contacted Wyatt who insisted she come in within the hour. The M.D. essentially shoved her out the door with nothing short of threats to appear "or else". The fact Wyatt was free concerned her since doctors never seemed to have time available within the actual calendar year, especially for new patients. She sat in the waiting room among the crying babies and loud children and mothers who looked as harassed as she. To Wyatt's credit, he saw her within thirty minutes, two minutes short of her losing her composure and calling the whole thing off. She explained as much to Bobby.

"But don't you need a second opinion?" he stressed.

"It'll be just as malignant with another doctor's biopsy. Bobby, I'm not shy. If I don't think it's going well, I'll seek a second opinion."

Bobby retreated from the role of pushy brother, "Just don't wait too long, 'kay?"

"I promise." Without saying it, her cousin was gently reminding her how Charlene waited and the consequences of that delay. "I'm not waiting like Mama did."

She heard him blow out a breath, relieved she caught his drift, "Good. And if there's anything I can help with, call me or have Ennis let me know."

14

Dr. Wyatt was a round, bookish man with an irritating habit of staring over his glasses while addressing her. It felt more like sitting in the principle's office than her doctor's. Another unnerving aspect was she stood at least six inches taller than he and when they stood side by side it was difficult to take him seriously, at least until he said *the* word. The word malignant rang day and night since Christmas Eve and when she and Ennis sat in Wyatt's office it rushed to the forefront once again.

The doctor allowed no time for chitchat or many pleasantries. Once the introductions and handshakes were over, he busied himself fanning out printed images of her breast on his desk. He lined them neatly in a row like a tarot card reader. He removed a pen from the pocket of his white doctor's coat and used it as a pointer, "This is the malignancy."

His choice of words hit her cold. In the physician's thesaurus, surely there were other terms available. Tumor, lump, growth, thing, it… Anything but *malignancy*.

Upon first glance, the tumor seemed harmless enough – certainly not life threatening. In fact, to her untrained eye, her breast looked relatively normal.

The area he pointed to appeared small, he said, which led her to hope he wasn't lying or judgment-challenged on measuring tumors. In his usual starchy manner, he reiterated his plan to use radiation treatments if the cancer hadn't spread, "if" being the key word. Best case scenario was radiation. The daily treatments would last around six weeks. If the cancer spread, he planned to start with chemotherapy followed by radiation.

Savannah recoiled. He wasn't much on bedside manner when it came down to business. If he'd seen her emotional turmoil the past few days, Wyatt would have either rephrased it or ducked. *He* didn't have the time bomb inside him. *He* didn't have to wonder if he'd survive after surgery and treatments. *He* didn't have to worry about his spouse or family if the treatments failed and he died.

You're tougher than a one eared alley cat, R.J. sometimes said. She supposed he meant it as a term of endearment since he usually smiled when he said it. That day, the last thing she felt was tough. She faced treatments for weeks on end knowing they'd drain her energy and shorten her temper.

Ennis put a gentle hand to her shoulder and gave it a squeeze. Now there was a sensitive man. Despite the cynical, no-nonsense view people had of cops, Ennis Rutherford broke the mold. Like any cop, he had his moments but with her, his tenderness and love shined brighter than the summer sun.

Savannah covered his hand with hers as Wyatt estimated the duration of the surgery from one to three hours. Again using his pen, he drew an imaginary line across a small area of one photo, "I'll make an incision over the malignancy and cut it out along with a small layer of tissue surrounding the tumor."

Savannah's knees went weak. Ennis physically steadied her, eased her into a chair. Dr. Wyatt sympathized, "I know it's a lot of information and it's overwhelming. If you're more comfortable not discussing the procedure –"

"No," she assured. "I need to know. Go ahead." She felt the doctor sizing up her expression. No doubt the same expression as hundreds or thousands of women displayed every day upon hearing they had breast cancer. She felt like someone ripped the rug from under her, leaving her flailing for stability – a stability found only with Ennis.

Dr. Wyatt continued, "After I remove the tumor and tissue, I'll take a sentinel node biopsy." He went on to explain the sentinel lymph node was the first lymph node or gland to receive lymphatic drainage from a tumor. Examination of the sentinel node was performed to learn whether that node did or did not contain tumor cells within it. "If that comes back negative, the cancer hasn't spread which means the radiation treatments will be our best bet. I realize having the treatments every day isn't anyone's idea of a party but you should probably anticipate the fatigue factor in your work. The longer the treatment goes, the more fatigue will set in and it will take several weeks to recoup your energy."

"I've," she cleared her throat to hopefully eliminate the building emotion, "informed my boss of the situation. He's letting me work at a desk instead of so much legwork." Truthfully, the decision to return to work still hung in the balance. She and Ennis mutually decided to table the discussion until after the surgery, when she was able to measure her physical capabilities better. Nevertheless, telling Dr. Wyatt that fact didn't set well with her, not right now.

The doctor nodded, pleased, "Consider taking some time off after the surgery. I'd like to see you take a couple of weeks if possible. At least until your follow up appointment."

"I've already scheduled two weeks off."

"Good and another thing. You'll stay overnight at the hospital. It's standard with me. Other surgeons allow the patient to go home the same day. I like the extra time to examine the incisions, see how they're doing. It will take a few days for the biopsy results." He gave her a moment to mentally digest the information.

Nausea boiled in her stomach. So much information and so little time to react. Neither Wyatt or Ennis saw Charlene's face or her weakness as the disease spread through her body. They couldn't picture her once plump cheeks and happy smile withering and fading as the cancer progressed. They never felt the frail grasp of a woman who stood up to a drunk, abusive husband and tried her best to raise three kids alone. They weren't there when Savannah got a tearful call from Georgia beckoning her sister to come *now* or risk not saying goodbye to their mother. Savannah raced at speeds that, on a normal day, would have terrified her. She ran into the hospital, pushing people aside in an attempt to see her mother before she passed away. She was ten minutes late.

Wyatt dealt with cancer every day, doling out bad news from eight to five. No matter how hard he tried, a certain amount of clinical detachment crept in for survival's sake. Being a cop, she understood the attempt to emotionally disengage while delivering bad news. But Ennis was there for her. The news hit him with the same impact it had her. It basically brought him to his knees. He hadn't suffered the pain of Charlene's struggle with cancer but he was here now, providing her daughter support and love that she and Georgia gave their mother. The tender squeeze on her shoulders as he stood behind her meant the world to her. Savannah reached back, took his hand in hers. Cradling it against her cheek, she tried to ground herself in his boundless strength. "I can still work during the treatments though, right?" she asked. "Since I'm on limited duty?"

"Of course. Just prepare yourself for the weakness during your treatment. You should get to bed earlier and maybe take a nap during the day. You may also get nauseated from the radiation."

"She won't mention it," Ennis eased into the subject, "but she's wondering about hair loss."

Dr. Wyatt nodded as though anticipating the question, "Unlike chemotherapy, radiation only affects the treated area. And I don't know many women who like much hair on their chest so it's not exactly a negative side effect."

Breathing a mental sigh of relief, Savannah smiled. She never found the right phrasing to say it. In his usual diplomatic manner, Ennis broached the concern but finessed his tone for minimal damage. Savannah hated to tell him but blunt, in this case, would have been fine with her. The time for diplomacy passed long ago. She wanted all the details good or not.

She mentioned hair loss twice to Ennis and he'd correctly presumed that it worried her more than she admitted. She figured she sounded vain by wanting to know.   Dr. Wyatt proved he was more in tune with her fears than she realized, "Savannah, everyone asks that question so don't feel bad. If you have any other questions, I'm here to answer them." He reached in his desk drawer for a sheet of paper. He visually skimmed it like a teacher grading a test, circling certain areas, marking through others.   He extended it to her, "Here's some information on how to combat the fatigue. Drink plenty of fluids and eat a healthy diet. Try to balance your activities, find a happy medium especially at work. Don't work to the point of exhaustion. I know your job has long hours and most times promotes a bad diet. Don't fall into that. Exercise in small amounts. No marathons for a while," he joked.

She laughed a little but the information overload mired her down like sinking in quicksand.

"Take advantage of offers to help," he continued.   "You mentioned a sister and brother. If they offer to cook or clean or run errands for you, don't refuse their help.   You need to take time to heal and it *will* take time. You'll both need time. As you see at the bottom of the page, I like for my patients to supplement their diet with high calorie foods or nutritional supplements to maintain their weight. Sometimes radiation causes a loss of appetite and patients who lose weight are more prone to fatigue. You're at a good weight now, don't drop any more."

"What about kids?" The words shot out before she managed to reclaim them. As evidenced by the men's expressions, she hadn't just opened Pandora's Box, she'd blown it apart.

"Kids?" her husband virtually squeaked. "You're wanting kids?"

A sign of humor relaxed Wyatt's features, "I was curious how long it would take you to mention it."

"You want kids?" Ennis seemed stuck on the same words. She hadn't intended to stun him. She merely wanted information for the future.

She tilted back and addressed his upside-down expression, "At some point, yes. Don't you?"

"Anytime you're ready."

Savannah returned to her original conversation, "Can I still have kids after the radiation?" Her voice softened to a near whisper, "You know, the long term side effects…"

Dr. Wyatt's fingers steepled beneath his chin, "There should be no problems in that area however I highly recommend you wait until I release you before you try achieving that particular goal."

15

The morning before the surgery, the gray sky parted, leaving behind a bright, cloudless, and more cheerful day. The sun's brilliant rays melted residual ice from sidewalks and warmed the day to a more temperate fifty-three degrees. Savannah awoke happy because of it and that itself delighted Ennis. He soon discovered why his wife rolled out of bed with a smile on her face. She and Georgia made plans to go shopping.

Georgia pulled up in her Tahoe just before ten that morning. The two left shortly after, their itinerary including Lenox Square Mall, Phipps Plaza and – time permitting – the Mall of Georgia.

Ennis wasn't a fool and he was damn sure his wife wasn't. They both suspected Georgia planned the outing to not only occupy Savannah's mind but her time. In the process, the walking provided exercise while the laid-back conversation supplied a seriously needed break from the upcoming surgery and other sensitive subjects.

For the past few days, they'd fielded phone calls from their colleague John Mathis and captain Josh Hunter. Those, along with her immediate family and his kept Savannah busy and weary of cancer talk. Then Bobby called again followed by a cousin named Grace. Linda tried on a regular basis but Ennis made various excuses for why his wife was never quite available. Every time the phone rang, he raced to check Caller ID. After a time, Savannah let him screen the calls without arguing. In retrospect, she hadn't put up much of a fight, probably *because* of Linda's last call.

While the girls were gone, he used the time for two important tasks. One, he reviewed Savannah's will since she'd asked him to. He had to brace himself for the task because sifting through his wife's final requests hardly put him in a cheerful mood.

During the lull of calls, he took advantage of the silence. After pouring a cup of coffee, Ennis sat at the dining table, unfolded the document and began reading the formal, impersonal legal jargon one page at a time.

The house, the car, the financials all went to him and as she stated, the orchards were left to him. Besides knowing nothing about fruit except how to peel an orange, he prayed never to own the orchards outside Augusta. He'd seen the massive tract of land brimming with rows of apple and peach trees and the newer addition of pecan orchards. Several years ago, Savannah told him, she and Georgia and the other cousins bought more land for the pecan endeavor and from the monetary return, the investment was worthwhile. As successful as the orchards were, he had no want for them. All he wanted was his wife to be okay.

In the will, Savannah also designated a few things to Seth if he wanted them. Other specific items went to Georgia, mostly glassware belonging to their mother and grandmother.

It was Lindsey's list that choked him down in details. Savannah planned to leave the little girl a virtual truckload of Charlene's things. She'd forewarned Ennis about the amount but explained since they didn't have kids yet, she wanted Lindsey to inherit her mother's things. When they had kids, she'd amend the will, she explained. The word "when" certainly wasn't lost on Ennis...

After reading the will, he decided to call Seth. While Georgia busied Savannah with shopping, Ennis sought answers to his wife's nightly torment. Since the diagnosis, he'd awakened her from terrors that not only made her cry and groan but left her dripping with sweat. They left him literally scared to let her drift off to sleep.

He assumed the nightmares revolved around her diagnosis. The brutal reality broke his heart. She called for her mother in sleep, the sound of a lonely child searching for the reassurance and love only a mother could provide. During the day Savannah appeared calm and in control. Once asleep, she reverted to the little girl begging for her mother's comfort.

Ennis sensed her need to talk about Charlene, to verbalize the pain. He'd tried to nudge her into doing so. Each time he was met with a shake of the head and a raised hand to shush him. He decided to turn in a different direction – Seth. He wanted, *needed*, to know what visions haunted Savannah. Once Seth began explaining the nightmare of their mother's illness and how Savannah reacted to it, Ennis's concern increased considerably. His wife had retreated to alcohol for an escape. Not just retreated, according to Seth, but lived in the bottle well after Charlene passed away.

Talking to Seth, he gained a new perspective on Savannah's

reaction to the news – and pretty much understood that reaction.

Ennis searched the cabinets for any bottles of bourbon but found none. Clearly his wife made a concerted effort to abstain. Now it was up to him to ensure she maintained total sobriety. After that show of temper at Georgia's house, he wanted nothing to do with that side of Savannah again. Fear literally flooded his veins at the drastic change in her personality. It wasn't so much her anger but the look in her eyes. It was a look he recognized with R.J. which, in a nice way, he labeled "dangerous".

Georgia and Savannah returned around three that afternoon – a short time after he completed his search for liquor. Various sizes of bags from every conceivable department store loaded their arms. Georgia could barely see over her purchases which he assumed to be bath towels and/or sweats. Savannah's sister kept them in enough bath towels that they ran out of room in the linen closet and now resorted to cramming the overflow in the hallway closet. As it were, she swamped them with four more for Christmas. He had no clue where they'd store those...

Ennis prayed the enormous bag held new sweats for them. They both enjoyed running in Piedmont Park and the sweats came in handy – much handier than another pile of bath towels.

Despite the armloads of sacks walking past him, he relaxed at Savannah's exuberant demeanor as, after she kissed him, she rattled off the various things they'd run across. Their credit cards might be crying for mercy but his wife was ecstatic. That alone was priceless.

She retired to the bedroom to change clothes. Georgia relieved herself of the bags she toted inside, "She bought a few things for you.

You'll like 'em."

"Anything Dallas Cowboys perhaps?" he inquired hopefully.

She wagged a finger at him, "She swore me to secrecy but nice try anyway."

Ennis leaned closer, "I need your help."

Georgia sat a huge Macy's sack on the floor. The resounding thud told Ennis they'd better start planning an addition to their little house to accommodate more towels.

"What do you need?" she asked.

He hated mentioning the subject since the two looked beyond euphoric upon entering the house. For days the issue bothered him and when he inquired about the drinking, Savannah refused to discuss it. He was desperate for answers and hated to go behind her back for them. In this case he had no choice. After giving the bedroom door a cautionary glance, he said in a hushed voice, "I need to know how bad her drinking problem is. I talked to Seth and he led me to believe she's on R.J.'s path."

Georgia's brow sank between her green eyes. He wasn't sure if she struggled to balance her reply toward the diplomatic side or was honestly at a loss for words. He got the distinct impression certain memories flashed in her mind, all of them unpleasant. She began speaking but focused on the Macy's sack instead of him, "Seth is sorta right but sorta wrong," she said, keeping her voice to a near whisper. "Savannah drank and most times you could tell it too." Now she looked at him, "She wasn't stumbling drunk, Ennis, that's not what happened. She drank enough to dull Mama's illness in her mind and when she sobered up, it all crashed in."

The bedroom door opened and Savannah stepped out in jeans and an old emerald green sweatshirt. Ennis recognized it as one of her "comfortable" shirts that saw no light of day except for housework or yard work. She breezed by him on her way to the kitchen. She kissed him as she passed, "I'm getting Grandma's dishes for Georgia so she can take 'em home."

He hoped she hadn't picked up on the conversation between him and her sister. By Georgia's nervousness, she fretted about it too, "Don't worry about it today, hon. There'll be another time."

Savannah's smiling face peeked around the corner, "No time like the present. It won't take that long to pack 'em up."

Ennis heard her wrestling the stepladder from the utility closet, "Need me to help?"

"Nope," she replied. "I need to keep busy anyway. Thanks for offering."

He heard her climb the stepladder then the cabinet door creak open. Once he heard the subdued clatter of dishes being moved, he leaned to Georgia and spoke softly, "I'm worried she'll start drinking again."

Georgia's hands fidgeted and her vision darted around like a nervous squirrel. She didn't outright refuse to talk about it but her expression implored him to drop the subject, "Just watch her, Ennis. That's all I can say." She whispered to him, "Besides Daddy's problem, there's one big reason she shouldn't drink. It intensifies her temper where anything sets her off and if she loses it, she really loses it."

Ennis nodded from reflex, remembering how his wife reared back to slap the living hell out of him. Had that hand connected, he'd have sported a red mark and probably a bruise. The brandy changed her personality to a darker side he prayed never to see again. He was just grateful Savannah gathered her wits quickly to realize what she'd tried to do. Her apology came from her heart and was sincere in every way. Listening to Georgia, Ennis concluded had Savannah consumed more than a few swallows, that apology might not have come at all.

Ennis sensed movement behind him. Georgia's wide eyes aimed around his shoulder told him they'd been caught. He dreaded facing his wife. He turned anyway and prepared himself for a firestorm.

Savannah stood with hands on hips, her cheeks flushed not from exertion but ire. Her elation from the shopping trip evaporated. Fierce resentment replaced it, "I neglected to realize the importance of this subject but since you're that interested in my past, I'll tell you all about it."

She'd hurled the words at him like rocks. He supposed he deserved it. Until Christmas Eve, he hadn't particularly suspected his wife ever drank a drop. Now she caught him sneaking behind her back, treating her like a liar or worse – a drunk like her father.

Georgia felt it her duty to explain, "Honey, he's concerned is all."

Savannah shifted her blue eyes to her sister, "I realize that but he shouldn't be asking you about it." Then they pinned Ennis again, "Did you talk to Seth too?"

Ennis could only half-shrug for an answer. His wife was about to blow her top. She had two degrees of temper – red hot or simmering. Currently she simmered with the temperature soaring straight to boil.

To his surprise, she merely sighed as her own shoulders lost the tension, her arms crossed over her chest.

He defended himself, "You always put me off when I mention it. I didn't know what else to do."

"I guess trusting me never occurred to you."

Ouch. That one struck right in the heart. His brain screamed the fact he played the same card she did about the biopsy. He tried to protect her like she had him. Only he had the distinct feeling the point would be completely lost on her right now, "I do trust you and you're right. I should have kept nagging you instead of asking Georgia or Seth. I'm sorry."

The apology seemed to help. Her voice lost its edge and so did her expression, "For the record, I don't exactly glow with joy when I revisit those days but had I known you'd interrogate my family about it, I'd have answered your questions."

"Hon, don't get upset with him," her sister urged in a gentle tone.

Savannah ventured closer to the pair, "I was hoping my past was just that. My past. But now I know why Grandma's dishes are arranged differently in the cabinet."

In his journey around the house, he tried to place everything back as he found it. He feared in his haste he forgot to replace something in its respective spot. Savannah wasn't a neat freak per se but things had their rightful places and she hated for them to be moved. She'd notice the cookie jar askew after Lindsey's visits or the ivy sitting on the counter was turned a different direction. The woman had eyes like a hawk.

Savannah's accusing inflection told him he'd been caught *again*.

Without another step, she seared him with a withering scowl, "You pilfered the cabinets thinking I stashed a bottle."

"Oh boy," Georgia muttered then stepped away, a move that highly concerned Ennis. It prompted images of running for the door, or at the very least, hiding Savannah's gun. Georgia treated him like a veritable leper which screamed the fact he'd overstepped his bounds so far he probably bailed off an invisible cliff.

"I'll be going," the older sister offered, "so you can work this out."

"No. Stay." Ennis nearly ended it with a "please". He felt cornered by his wife and now felt abandoned by an ally.

Savannah agreed, "He'll feel better if you stay." In a brief spark of anger, she fisted her hands but kept her arms crossed, "Ennis, I told you I didn't keep liquor in the house. Do you believe me now?"

He nodded in silence. She was so close to him, the heat of her temper rolled off her in waves. Her cheeks flushed dark red, contrasting against her blue eyes. Then, in a complete change of character, she sighed again and headed to the coffee pot.

Ennis heard her pouring one cup then another. A spoon clinked inside the ceramic cup while she stirred cream and sugar in her coffee. She rounded the corner holding two mugs. She handed the black coffee to Georgia then sat down, "When Mama was diagnosed I couldn't cope and started drinking. When she died, I drank more because I thought it helped. So for the funeral, I fortified myself real well and ended up embarrassing myself because Linda and her ilk spurred me into reacting."

"Anyone would have reacted to the awful things they said," Georgia replied.

Ennis saw the lines in his wife's brow ease slightly upon her sister's justification. He was clueless to whatever they spoke of but neither seemed eager to divulge details.

Savannah continued, "My temper's worse when I drink. I get aggressive and physical like Daddy." In a slow, deliberate move, she lifted the mug and took a sip. What began as a clinical account evolved into a tug-of-war between showing emotion or closing it away. As promised, she waded through the difficult period of her life but did it without looking him in the eyes. She fixated on the will before her and spoke slowly and clearly but not once did her vision meet his.

Ennis sat across from her, gave her time to think, to regroup. Georgia eased into the seat beside her. He saw the older sister focus on the will. She said nothing.

"Linda said horrible things about Mama and Daddy. She, Abby and Teresa ganged up on Seth, Georgia and me. What they said…" Tears glistened in her eyes, "Linda said she was glad Mama was gone, that it was better she was dead than living the life she had." Savannah met his vision, her teeth clenched against the rising anger, "She said it with a damn smile. They were all jealous of Mama because she married into a little more money than their mothers did."

Georgia's hand covered hers and gently squeezed, her voice offering its own comfort, "Stop feeling guilty. You were defending Mama and Daddy."

"I was half drunk and the three of 'em set me off so I hauled off and hit Linda," Savannah smiled as she relived the satisfaction, "She stumbled back into Abby's arms. I nearly knocked all three of 'em down with that one punch, just like a domino fall. I went after Linda again and it took Daddy and Seth to pull me off. I wasn't giving up until those three were dead or gone."

Her vision tried to meet his but couldn't quite make it, "Anyway, that's one of my most embarrassing moments. After the funeral, I got worse because I missed Mama. I drank on and off through the academy. My first partner warned me about drinking and when I wrecked one night, I decided he was right, that I had shit for brains."

Georgia turned toward her so fast Ennis thought her head might spin off her neck. The older sister sounded as surprised as he felt, "You never told me about a wreck."

Savannah wrapped her hands around the coffee cup, warming them. If it were anyone else, Ennis might have thought she was stalling but with Savannah, he knew she gathered her courage.

"Riley, my first partner, was a good cop. He was just hard on me sometimes. Looking back, I deserved it. One day, he'd ridden me hard about a mistake I'd made. I didn't follow protocol on one stop and it pissed him off. After shift, I sat in my car and brooded and drank. I was pretty drunk when I drove home. I was speeding and probably weaving. I rounded the south side of Morningside Drive at about forty or fifty –"

Georgia's gasp halted her temporarily and Savannah glanced at Ennis. His jaw, he was sure, dragged the floor. Morningside Drive wound through a heavily wooded area with trees lining both sides of the road. The speed limit, for good reason was set at twenty. His blood ran cold as he imagined her car barreling around the corners at nearly fifty.

"I skidded across both lanes – thankfully the coast was clear so no head-on collision – and crashed into a tree. It was a miracle I didn't kill someone."

He felt like a chump. She'd come in from shopping in a cheerful mood and less than thirty minutes later, she scraped bottom. The lone positive aspect of the confession ended up being something totally surprising. He now understood her abhorrence of drunk drivers. He assumed it revolved around her father. Instead it revolved around her own bad choices. Memories of the accident where Hayley and her mother died took on a new meaning. *Leave that bastard for last. He's the reason this whole thing happened*, she'd said. The hatred in her voice struck him as peculiar upon later recollection. Now it made perfect sense. "Were you hurt?" he wanted to know.

Shame crossed her features, "Not really. A few bumps and scrapes like that bastard the other night. That's the thing about drunks, I've noticed. They kill or maim other people when they drive but they usually walk away just fine. That night I realized how close I came to hurting any number of innocent people."

During that time, Georgia's aggravation peaked, "That's what happened to your car? You told me –"

"It seemed less awkward than fessing up that I was stone drunk and slammed into a tree." She looked back to Ennis, "That's when I had to buy another car. I vowed to sober up and I did."

"There had to be a police report," he hinted gently. He pushed the subject further than she probably expected him to. But an accident caused by a drunken cop had to be addressed to some extent...

Savannah met his gaze. By the icy stare, he wished she'd have continued averting her eyes. He vowed to back off if she chose to explain the police report. One more question and he might sport a bruise similar to what she'd laid on Linda years before.

Thankfully after a few seconds, her blue eyes softened, "I called Riley from a pay phone. He called a tow truck and informed me that after he took care of the paperwork, he was putting in for a different partner. I begged him not to, that I'd straighten up if he'd give me another chance. He didn't believe me but agreed anyway. I did fine until I testified at Terence LaVeau's trial and saw what he'd done to those little girls. I blamed myself for their deaths. Still do. Especially Rachel Ballard. I knew Terence was a bastard."

"You couldn't have known what your new partner was up to," Ennis reasoned.

Georgia agreed, "No one knew, Savannah. None of the other officers and not his boss. Not even his mother, if I remember correctly."

Savannah shook her head, "Doesn't make it any easier to deal with. I tried to save Rachel. She was standing right behind him. I tried but he overpowered me."

Ennis sensed she fought back tears. He was right. Her voice struggled to stay steady, "Being a cop isn't worth it at times. What you see and experience changes you and not for the better in most cases. Keeps you from trusting people then when you find someone to love and trust, you spend all your time worrying you'll lose them because you've seen what can happen." She looked directly at Ennis, wiped a tear, "I don't want to lose you. Not because of the job or drinking or whatever. You've shown me what true love can be and what it means to love a person with everything they have. I never thought I'd love anyone as much as I love you."

16

Ennis rubbed his forehead. The damn headache hadn't let up since Christmas Eve. It started after Savannah confessed to the discovery and biopsy, lingered through the holiday, pestered him the day at Dr. Wyatt's office then laid in heavy the day of her surgery.

Once they wheeled his wife through the surgery doors, the family migrated to the waiting room. He found no respite there either. Two TVs blared from the corners, one with Jeopardy, the other with CNN. Kids ran amuck, screaming and giggling and the nearby parents neglected to call them down or control them. The den of voices rose to combat the loud TVs and kids, all of which added to his general distress.

Ennis decided it was time to accept Georgia's offer of two aspirin and a bottle of water. He saw her dig through her purse to fetch the aspirin. What he really waited to see was if she carried a bottle of water somewhere in the depths of the large leather handbag. She did.

Dane leaned in to whisper, "You'd be amazed what that woman can carry in that itty bitty thing."

He supposed he would even though the purse wasn't as "itty bitty" as Dane thought. It looked sizeable enough to carry a woman's usual belongings plus a couple or three paperbacks. Savannah carried hers under her arm or carried a small shoulder bag. They were only big enough to contain the bare essentials plus her badge if need be.

Once the aspirins hit bottom, he sighed, praying they worked quick. He rubbed his temple again. Surveying the crowd around him, his headache temporarily eased. All the right people came to support Savannah. Her cousin Bobby arrived before the surgery as well as Mathis and their captain. They hung around until leaving for work. That left Ennis, his mother, Dane, Georgia and Seth and his family, all sitting in a tight little group – farthest from Jeopardy or CNN though not nearly far enough away from the screaming children.

Taking stock of himself, he realized he looked more like a vagrant than a concerned husband. Everyone around him presented a bright-eyed and stylish appearance while he settled for sleepless and rumpled. He grabbed the first thing he stumbled across that morning which happened to be an azure blue button-down shirt and a pair of well worn jeans. He'd shaved and combed his hair while Savannah showered then the two hit the road to the hospital.

The rest of the assembled group put him to shame. Adults and children all dressed up – not down like he – and their faces showed signs of actual rest. Lindsey and Dylan busied themselves with the coloring books and crayons Leah brought.

His and Dane's mother, of course, brought her knitting. She wielded the foot long needles with deadly precision and claimed the twiddling of them eventually would produce a sweater. Ennis suspected it was another Christmas present. The yarn of choice was purple this time and he wondered if the sweater wasn't meant for Savannah or perhaps Georgia.

Studying Seth's behavior, Ennis concluded Savannah's brother made worrying a hobby. He either paced back and forth or worried with his wedding ring when tension mounted. For now he settled on staring at his children's work while twirling the gold band on his finger.

Dane had Georgia and Georgia had Dane. They held each other's hands and comforted each other while making sure to include him or check on his mood. Ennis knew the two were destined for a wedding. He'd bet any amount of money on it.

"Anyone want a cup of coffee?" Georgia asked everyone.

Ennis immediately looked at her handbag, "If you pull one outta that purse, I'm gonna drop dead of surprise."

She chuckled, "It carries a lot but not that much. I'll go get us some coffee."

"I'm fine, really. But thanks." The rest declined as he had. If the surgery ran into the second hour, he'd probably need a quart of coffee just to keep busy. He couldn't help but think how much easier life was as a bachelor. It was also considerably lonelier. He'd heard his daddy describe love to him, how being in love hurt like hell but, at the same time, felt finer than anything imaginable. "You'll know when you're in love," he'd said. "At times you'll feel addled, sweaty, weak in the knees and a little unscrewed too."

"The flu does the same thing," Ennis had replied as though falling in love was nothing short of catching the plague.

His daddy smiled, "But this is one ailment you'll never want cured."

His daddy was right. The instant he saw Savannah, he was thunderstruck. The adage "love at first sight" – an adage Ennis discounted as fluff – proved to be real. He went on his merry way, single and happy, until this beautiful creature entered his life. His goal changed from starting fresh in a new city to marrying Savannah Prince. He found himself arriving early to work. He walked her to her car, took her to lunch and dinner if she allowed. His hours without her were cold, empty. During their off hours he called to shoot the breeze, discuss their current case, anything to hear her voice. At last she broached his constant attention by asking, "They don't have women in Texas, do they?" Her subsequent smile gave him hope that she felt an attraction to him as well.

In her he saw Scarlett's fire and independence with an abundance of Melanie's love, loyalty and gentleness. Savannah's tough exterior fell away in his presence, giving way to a generous, soft-hearted – and sometimes whimsical – soul that emerged only when in the company of certain people. She played Scarlett's role at work, blustering and bullying suspects and charming uniform cops to get her way. With him, she evolved to a spunkier version of Melanie with a liberal sprinkling of Miss Scarlett thrown in for good measure.

Ennis glanced at his watch. She'd been in surgery thirty minutes. Love was hell on a person. Savannah was his life, his soul. He could protect her from gunfire, disreputable relatives and some doped up bastard taking a swing at her. But he couldn't protect her from breast cancer. Ennis never felt so helpless in his life.

Before they wheeled her into surgery, she presented a strong front for her audience. In private, Ennis saw the fear in her eyes. He clasped her hand, kissed it and with his vow of love, her anxiety eased and she relaxed. To love a woman so wholly was the greatest high when things went well and the deepest wound when they ran aground.

"She'll be back soon, Ennis." Georgia reached over and patted his hand.

He tried to smile, "I just miss her."

"I know one thing. That kid is nuts over you." Seth leaned onto his knees like Ennis, "She's a lot easier to get along with since she's married. You've managed to calm her down more than Mama could. But when she died, Savannah's temper got worse. There was one time..."

Leah cleared her throat then gestured to the kids, "Little pitchers..."

Up to that point, the kids had been coloring at a nearby coffee table. Now, both kids sat with crayons in hand, staring saucer-eyed at their father. Seth's tone gave Ennis pause as well. By the end, he sounded disgusted with Savannah.

Lindsey practically idolized her aunt and Ennis felt a rising resentment toward Seth for lashing out. No one was perfect, he wanted to say, but don't tear into Savannah in front of Lindsey. Neither of them deserved it.

Realizing his blunder, Seth waved off the rest of his rant, "That was a long time ago. She's better thanks to Uncle Ennis."

Leah basically steamrolled her husband with a scathing look. She conveyed the same words Ennis craved to. Shut up and play nice. Seth leaned back and sighed.

Ennis checked his watch then rubbed his other temple.   He expected the headache to last a minimum of five years until she was declared cancer free. No amount of aspirin or banging his head against a wall would ease it.

"Honey, she'll be fine," his mother assured. "It takes time for the surgery then she'll be in recovery for a while."

An empathetic half-smile graced Georgia's Rita Hayworth features, "Ennis, please calm down."

"Yeah," Dane added, "or you'll be ridin' a gurney yourself. Ain't no good to Savannah if you're passed out cold."

Calming down wasn't scheduled until, oh, roughly three months from now.   There were plenty of hurdles to overcome before that. Surgery, test results, follow-up appointments, treatments…   Besides all that he worried about Savannah's emotional state, her ability to cope with whatever the results were.   She needed his strength.   Allowing his concerns and fears to surface had to wait – if possible – but they plagued him day and night like festering thorns.   What if the tumor spread? What if she required chemotherapy?   What if *nothing* worked and her situation was just like her mother's?

He refused to actively entertain the negative thoughts since his wife possessed amazing intuition. She could detect the slightest nuance of negative energy from people around her.   She could also spot a patronizing statement from a mile off.   And sympathy?   God help the poor soul who attempted to convey that.

Ennis checked his watch once more.   An hour passed.   His thoughts wandered to the job. Would she retire? Not likely, at least not yet. She needed her normal routine and the job gave her that, even if she stayed on limited duty.

He readjusted in his seat. The chairs were too hard, he reflected with a wince and it felt like summertime inside the crowded waiting room. He broke a sweat and his hands were clammy. Someone jacked the heat up and for a nickel he'd turn the damn thing off just to finally breathe again. He referred to his watch which annoyingly hadn't moved but two minutes since his last peek. Now he knew how caged animals felt.

The kids grew antsy, no doubt because of his squirming. They spent half their time coloring, the other half watching him. The second they had laid eyes on his mother, they'd welcomed her like a cherished grandmother, lavishing her in stories of recent events in their lives. Mama sat, riveted by each word and responding in kind to each precious nugget of information.

Dylan bragged on the lizard he caught and moped that his mom refused to let him keep it. Lindsey boasted about the new fish Santa brought and "the big ol' fish tank" Savannah gave her for Christmas. With a prance to her step, she announced that she was to be Savannah's official nurse during her recuperation. Mama Rutherford was sufficiently impressed.

Still sandwiched between his brother and a table covered in golf magazines, Ennis busied himself writing notes and referring to the papers Dr. Wyatt gave them Monday. He began jotting a list for Kroger's, beginning with the nutritional supplements the doctor insisted she drink.

Dane leaned closer, "What's all that?"

"Gotta pick this up at Kroger's. He wants her to drink this stuff so she doesn't get too tired or lose weight." He rubbed at his temple, the enormity of their upcoming battle sinking in hard. "And she drops pounds pretty easy anyway. Can't imagine how hard it'll be to sustain her weight when she doesn't feel like eating."

Georgia touched his arm, lifting his frown to her composed features, "Ennis, we'll pick up what you need. I have a key to your place so Dane and I can put things away." She gifted him with a smile that told him to relax, "Stop worrying so much. If she loses her appetite, I'll keep her in peach pies and ham sandwiches. Nothing keeps her away from those."

He returned the smile, thanking her. The whole state of affairs confounded him. What did one do for someone with breast cancer? What could he say to ease Savannah's concern? He knew how sensitive the subject was and how important healthy, normal breasts were to a woman's identity and pride. Ennis laid awake nights thinking of ways to help Savannah cope. And the instant she was fit for making love, God help her because he could barely keep his hands to himself lately. If she feared his love waned with this illness, she'd soon find out the opposite.

A male voice boomed down the hospital hallways, growing closer and louder by the second, "Her given name is Savannah Charlene Prince but she went and got married and I don't know what the hell her name is now."

Ennis's hackles rose. Not only the room's heater but now his temper made him sweat. He wiped the damp perspiration from his brow *again* as anger and alarm coursed through his body. The last thing they needed was R.J.. The old man made a living creating hell for anyone around him and this was possibly the worst time for him to show up. Ennis clamped his lips tight for fear blistering expletives might fall from them. The last thing he wanted was to upset Savannah's siblings or alienate Seth's children. Plus, his mother wouldn't exactly react kindly to the words struggling for freedom.

Georgia instantly cowered at Ennis's boiling animosity, "I'm sorry, Ennis. I called Daddy but I never thought he'd show."

He swallowed the sincere desire to give her a piece of his mind. Savannah clearly informed everyone to keep R.J. out of her business. Ennis just sighed. He knew Georgia would be the one to botch up the plans. Savannah would spit fire when she saw R.J. and Ennis couldn't blame her.

Seth rose from his seat, motioned for Georgia to follow. He calmly addressed the others, "Pardon us, please. We'll be back shortly."

Ennis chanced a glance behind him. From the corner of his eye, he saw R.J. searching the numerous faces in the room, looking for anyone familiar, "'Ja hear me? Where's my baby? Her name is –"

The boisterous voice suddenly ceased – Ennis assumed because of Seth. Savannah's brother had a way of shutting people up without uttering a syllable. Today, Ennis appreciated his effort.

People stared, some recoiling from the rowdy, burly drunk, others shot him fiery glares hot enough to melt glass.

A period of silence punctuated by a low but neutral voice – Seth's – did little to assuage R.J.'s anger, "Where's that boy that roped her into marriage? I wanna talk to *him*. She was fine till she hooked up with him. Wha'd he do to her?"

Seth voiced another composed yet indecipherable reply. Mama Rutherford, on the other hand, bristled. The last thing they needed was her on the warpath. His mother redefined the word anger when genuinely riled. Her gentle face evolved into an almost comical scowl – until she turned loose on a person. Then it wasn't so funny. If anyone stood a decent chance of successfully squaring off with R.J. Prince, it was Mama.

She bounded to her feet, her jaw set, "I've had enough of that talk," she said.

Dane and Ennis rose to meet her, "Don't do it, Ma," they both warned in unison. Ennis leaned closer, "I told you her daddy is a mean drunk. He's not above hitting anyone that makes him mad, including women."

She defended her actions, "I won't tolerate anyone speaking of you in that manner or tone."

"Ma, I understand, but he's a violent person and Seth and Georgia are trying to get him outta here quietly."

Dane took his mother's hand, his other arm sliding across her shoulders, "Sit down, Ma. Let them handle it."

Leah touched her other arm and nodded, "It's hard to accept but you finally do. R.J. isn't someone you tangle with, Mrs. Rutherford." She pointed to Lindsey and Dylan whose wide-eyed stares volleyed between whoever spoke. "I'm pretty sure," Leah continued, "that the kids would enjoy your help with their pictures."

The fire in Mama's eyes flickered once more then diminished to an indignant flame. She sank back in the chair, her attention moving to the two children with crayons in hand. As though their astonished expressions broke her mood, she finally smiled and busied herself with admiring their work.

Ennis noticed the children's posture relaxed while he and Dane meandered toward the dividing wall between the two waiting rooms. Peeking around the corner, he saw Georgia and Seth flanking R.J., both speaking to him and, by his reaction, calming him down. Their father's face hadn't seen a razor in a week and his clothes appeared slept in. He hugged Georgia, kissed her cheek. He never offered to shake his son's hand. When R.J. stepped forward, he swayed slightly, forcing Georgia to steady him. Ennis's temper fully engaged. Their father drove directly from a bar in Augusta, he assumed, and endangered plenty of lives on the way. He ended up in the exact spot Savannah never wanted him to be: at the hospital during her surgery.

Ennis doubted Seth would allow R.J. to stay, particularly in his inebriated condition. First, Savannah didn't want him there and second, Seth's kids were present. Seth never allowed R.J. around his kids and that sparked endless fights between the two. In a perfect world, he'd leave but as life continued to prove, the world was anything but perfect.

"You think he'll leave?" Dane whispered over his brother's shoulder.

"I doubt it. Savannah is his 'baby' even though he treats her like dirt. He's not leaving."

Dane ducked, "Here they come."

Ennis didn't move, his ire still percolating, "Yeah. All three of 'em."

Georgia, Seth and R.J. made their way toward them, Georgia's face still lined with concern as her father leaned into her for support.

Seth's lips pressed together so tight they blanched as he stared after his father. When he passed Ennis, Seth whispered, "It's a trial run. I told him there are plenty of men here who will haul his ass out by his whiskers if he causes problems. Let's keep that promise."

Ennis nodded, "You can bet we will."

The surgery lasted nearly two hours. Ennis was pacing the floor by that time, wondering if they carted his wife to Brazil for the procedure. He wasn't the only nervous person. Dane took to biting his nails, Georgia to staring at the clock and Seth about twisted his wedding ring *and* finger off his hand and his mother's knitting began taking shape at an astronomical rate. R.J., on the other hand, sprawled out in a chair beside Seth and promptly fell asleep.

An hour later the group traveled upstairs to her assigned room, waiting for her return from recovery. Dane kept nibbling, Georgia continued staring and he started pacing again. Leah busied her husband by placing little Dylan in his lap while the boy nodded off to sleep like his grandfather.

The floor was alive with activity, nurses scurrying by the door, equipment rattling past and visitors arrived to see other patients in nearby rooms. With every round he paced, he poked his head out the door, checking for any signs of Savannah. He felt positive he looked like a prairie dog popping its head out of its hole to survey the surroundings.

"Honey, the doctor said about thirty minutes," his mother gently reminded.

He nodded. That wasn't all the doctor said. The tumor measured three centimeters. Ennis thought that was rather small and felt damned relieved over it. Then Wyatt added the five year survival rate was about ninety-two percent if the lymph nodes were cancer free, and sixty-three percent if more than three lymph nodes weren't. Ennis sat down before his knees caved. His brother put a hand to his shoulder, gave it a reassuring squeeze.

Dr. Wyatt saw Ennis's virtual collapse and tried to explain, "The results won't be back for a few days. There's no reason to begin worrying yet." That was easy for the doctor to say, Ennis thought. He hadn't fought tooth and nail to marry Savannah. He hadn't seen her struggle with the nightmares and the mental anguish of the diagnosis. The more Ennis mulled it over, the more agitation set in until he instructed everyone, "No one tells her about the sixty-three percent survival rate." He looked directly at R.J., "No one."

"Ennis, it doesn't mean that's her percentage," Leah reasoned.

"I know but she dwells on the negative for obvious reasons and I want her attitude positive going into the treatments. I'm looking at it from her perspective. She hears sixty-three, she'll think she's on the same road her mother took."

The clatter of wheels on tile caught his attention and when he emerged from the memory of Wyatt's announcement, he was biting his nails like his brother. Ennis raced to the door to see a bed being guided by two nurses. His wife resembled a little girl tucked beneath the blanket, fast asleep. It was the most peaceful he'd seen her in over a week.

He stepped aside, watched them steer the bed through the door and into the room. The noise roused Dylan. He blinked awake then blinked again. His vision focused somewhere over the bed, "Look," he pointed, "a bird."

Ennis and the others turned to where the boy pointed. Ennis saw nothing that remotely looked birdlike. A shadow from the window may have served as one but it was a healthy stretch of the imagination. Seth stood with his son in his arms, trying to shush him but the boy kept pointing, his cries insistent, "Birdie, birdie, birdie..."

Leah apologized on behalf of her enthusiastic son, "He's got a vivid imagination."

"And a loud mouth," Seth mumbled, setting him down.

Ennis moved his vision from Dylan to Lindsey whose eyes were rounded and aimed in the same direction her brother's finger pointed. Whatever "bird" Dylan thought he saw, Lindsey must have seen it too.

The family stood aside while nurses checked the IVs and straightened blankets around Savannah. Through the motions, she never moved. Her slow, even breathing signaled a restful sleep, something Ennis was grateful for.

A nurse touched her hand, "Savannah, your family's here."

Ennis's heart thundered in his chest in anticipation of seeing her beautiful blue eyes open. He wanted to tell her it all went well, that Dr. Wyatt sounded confident. He had so much to say, he practically burst to begin but there was one big problem. Savannah didn't open her beautiful blue eyes. In fact, she didn't stir at all so the nurse called her again.

Still nothing. To her chagrin, the nurse blushed from slight embarrassment, "She was awake in recovery. Kept asking for Ennis so she's just drifted off is all."

Drifted off? More like *sped off* to La La Land, he thought, and she neglected to leave a forwarding address. He figured the stress of everything along with the anesthesia conked her out good. At home, she slept fitfully and was restless to the point Ennis worried she'd never sleep again. Looking at his sleeping beauty, he smiled.

Georgia and R.J. crowded one side of the bed while Ennis rounded the other. He clasped her warm hand in his. His thumb caressed the delicate fingers resting in his palm. His other hand swept her hair back and Ennis placed a kiss to her forehead with a whispered vow of "I love you".

Savannah's eyes slowly moved beneath the lids. After great effort, they gradually opened to see her sister and father. "Mama?" was the throaty, lethargic question followed by, "Daddy?"

Ennis's heart broke. The hopeful tone accompanying "Mama" told him her vision wasn't yet clear. Until she focused, Georgia would continue looking like Charlene and after seeing photos of their mother, Ennis completely understood how a person confused the two. They looked incredibly alike.

Her greeting to R.J. sounded completely puzzled. She probably wondered how the hell he found out about her surgery. Once the cobwebs cleared, she'd realize Georgia informed him – and not be one bit happy about it. Bless Georgia's heart, she meant well but sometimes she screwed up big time. Savannah swore Ennis to secrecy regarding R.J. and he assumed she did the same with her siblings. He retracted the assumption. He flat-out *knew* she'd sworn them to secrecy and probably tacked on threats of bodily harm if they reneged.

Savannah blinked again, "Daddy?" Oh yes, there it was. A wisp of disbelief. One Georgia attempted to snuff out by saying, "Honey, you look so good. I doubt I'd look that good if I had surgery."

Undeterred, the patient's temper surfaced albeit muted, "What are you doing here?" she asked the unshaven man bending down to kiss her.

R.J. smiled a little. Ennis never liked it when he smiled. God forgive him, Robert Jefferson Prince made a simple smile look evil – or maybe it was because Ennis knew him too well...

Savannah winced with her father's peck on her cheek. With the week long beard bristling from his face and chin, Ennis figured it felt like someone smacked her with a cactus.

R.J.'s voice sounded amazingly proud, "Sweets called me and said you was having surgery. I wasn't about to let my baby go through it without me."

Ennis watched his wife's vision flick to Georgia whom she now recognized as her sister and not her mother. The whole room was privy to who "Sweets" was except Mama who stood beside Ennis. He neglected to inform his mother that R.J. pinned the nickname on Georgia while Savannah was "my baby". Seth had no nickname, he guessed, because R.J.'s only son basically disowned him.

"You told him?" Savannah croaked at her sister. Irritation mounted as consciousness set in. Judging by her distress, Georgia's treachery bit to the bone.

The older sister bent to whisper, "He's our father, like it or not.

Don't be angry. Mama wouldn't like it."

Ennis squeezed her hand, bringing her attention to him. Her eyes instantly lost their hardness and ire. Savannah brightened instantly and he smiled when she squeezed him back. He kissed her, "Hey there, beautiful. Dr. Wyatt said the surgery went well."

"Good, 'cause I don't intend to do it again," her fingers tightened around his. "I missed you."

Ignoring the narrow glare R.J. skewered him with, Ennis kissed her once more. He lingered at her ear, "I missed you too. I was completely lost without you."

"Yeah," Dane added, overhearing the sweet nothing, "and a certified basket case. Glad you're doing so well, Peach."

Savannah's smile broadened when her vision settled on Mama Rutherford. The older woman patted her knee, "Georgia's right, honey. You do look good. I'm sorry Dane and I are late. We wanted to be here before your surgery but the flight was delayed–"

"Storms *again*," Dane complained.

"Thank you both for coming," she said, the words still thick and leaden. "It's good to wake up and see you here."

Dylan's finger tapped at Savannah's calf. She searched for the source until Seth lifted his son again, "There you go, buddy. Now Aunt Savannah can see you."

Ennis listened to the exchange between Savannah and the boy. As expected, Dylan shied away upon first sight of her. No, she didn't particularly sound like her usual self. Her voice was slow, throaty and occasionally skipped a syllable. She didn't look like Dylan remembered either. He was accustomed to the vibrant, wise-cracking aunt that wore only enough makeup to highlight her features and kept her dark wavy hair either in a ponytail or free around her shoulders. In a remote sort of way, Ennis admitted, she looked like she'd been in battle and the winner was still in question.

Savannah smiled at him and after a brief exchange, Dylan warmed up to her, albeit bashfully.

The next candidate for conversation was Lindsey. Unlike her younger brother, she strode confidently to the bed. To Ennis, she possessed the appearance of a genuine nurse, not surprising since it was her mother's profession. "Don't worry 'bout nothin'," the girl stated proudly. She curled her long brown hair behind her ears, "Mama said I'm in charge now and I'm gonna help you get well."

Ennis had no doubt about that. By her expression, neither did Savannah. She gifted the girl with a smile, "So you're my new boss."

Leah perched a hand on Lindsey's shoulder, "She's memorized everything I told her to do."

Seth leaned in, "A word to the wise, sis. Never say no. Lindsey's like her mother and that word is unacceptable."

R.J. laid a hand on Savannah's calf, gave it a gentle squeeze, "They tell me you'll be havin' treatments after this." He ran a hand down his jaw, "There's just one thing I wanna say."

Ennis tensed. R.J. held his tongue until now. By the look on her father's face, his next words would be a doozy. Ennis felt Savannah's fingers tighten on his. She sensed it coming too. "What is it, Daddy?" she asked.

"You do what these doctors tell ya. Eat what ya gotta eat, drink what ya gotta drink, go where ya gotta go and get them treatments. 'Cause there's one thing I *don't* want ya to do. Don't die like your mama did."

17

Savannah never expected her father to be genteel. She never expected him to be eloquent with words or dress in the best clothes. But in her heart she honestly never expected him to lash out with such a blatantly hurtful collection of words as "don't die like your mama". His statement, she told Georgia later, was a prime example of why she begged for the simple concept of confidentiality.

Dealing with her mouthy sister was only one hurdle. Ennis threw in his contribution when they discussed her surgery. After arriving in her hospital room and she opened her eyes, she'd uttered her parent's names. Ennis found it particularly humorous, "You called Georgia 'Mama'." He must have seen her spark of annoyance because he concluded with, "But I knew your vision wasn't clear yet."

Savannah begged to differ. Her vision was fine. She recognized her sister and R.J. standing beside her but it was the third figure *behind* them that inspired the outburst. No older than thirty-five, Charlene's image smiled down at her youngest. After Savannah called her name, the likeness of her mother faded as Charlene waved to her.

The remembrance brought tears at times but the tears quickly dried, replaced with a comfort Savannah couldn't explain. But, in her opinion, at least she wasn't nuts. She did see her mother in that room. Savannah didn't argue with her husband nor did she correct Georgia when she giggled about the "mistake" her sister made.

In the days following the surgery, Georgia and Dane took turns either calling or dropping by, usually with food. Every day the older sister paraded a day's worth of provisions into the kitchen with instructions, "Just warm it in the oven or heat it in a skillet". Her sister needed a cause, Savannah supposed, and she was it.

"Can't keep the woman out of the kitchen," Dane mumbled with a frown. He stared down at his belly, "An' you can't keep me outta the food. I'll be so fat I'll have to buy two tickets to board the plane home."

Savannah knew the feeling. She'd probably gained ten pounds in three days from Georgia's culinary talents and couldn't care less. Besides Thanksgiving and Christmas, Savannah hadn't eaten so many excellent meals in such a short span of time. Her sister was a veritable genius when preparing anything involving pork. So besides casseroles, soups, steaks and baked chicken, Georgia included a number of pork dishes as well. Savannah made a note to go shopping for bigger jeans. At the rate she was eating, she'd be lucky to fit through the front door in the following weeks.

The second day Savannah was home, Lindsey surprised everyone by asking to spend the next few nights with her aunt and uncle. Seth and Leah debated over it, reasoning that Savannah didn't need the added stress of a child day and night. Stress wasn't the word Savannah would have used. Lindsey was a doll when the two were together. Sure she pitched miniature hissy fits but that came with the pedigree of being a Southern girl – and a Prince. Her tantrums lasted a few minutes then she opted to pout for an hour then, as with most kids, she was fine. They were nothing Savannah or Ennis couldn't handle. In fact, Savannah wanted to say, she needed the distraction of an energetic child, someone whose vocabulary included more talk of fish and school instead of cancer.

"Maybe when she's feeling better you can stay the night," Leah told her daughter.

Lindsey's dejection, her fallen expression and slumped shoulders tugged at Savannah. The little girl muttered a promise to "be good".

Savannah thought it time to rescue the child, "Lindsey will be fine. After all, she promised to take care of me and that's hard to do from across town."

The debate lasted another solid ten minutes until Seth trekked home to pack an overnight bag for his daughter. Leah stayed behind to instruct Lindsey on what to do and clearly emphasized what *not* to do while she was their guest.

Lindsey turned out to be the perfect houseguest. Savannah and Ennis tucked her into bed at nine o'clock sharp each night. Their niece stretched and yawned from a long day of fetching drinks and food for her aunt. Savannah hadn't the heart to tell her that her legs hadn't had surgery and that walking wasn't exactly a challenge. The youngster had a point to make, especially the next day when serving a drink that looked similar to chocolate milk. Savannah figured it was coming sooner or later. The nutritional supplements Dr. Wyatt prescribed now became part of her daily routine. Every day she took enough vitamins to choke a horse but Savannah decided to make the best of it, "What's this? A milkshake?" She slanted a sly grin at her niece, "Did you make it?"

Lindsey nodded, "'Specially for you. Uncle Ennis says you gotta take this too."

Her small hand dropped a pill in Savannah's palm. Another vitamin. She gave the pill a disparaging frown. How many damned healthy things were they forcing on her anyway?

"Gotta take it," Lindsey reminded.

"I gotta?"

The girl crossed her arms, her nod firm, "Gotta. Mama says it's good for you."

She crooked her finger at her niece, drawing her closer, "Normally I'd argue about somethin' I gotta do but because *you* think I should, I'll take it, especially since you brought a good ol' milkshake to wash it down."

Lindsey broke into a wide grin. The girl's efforts did more than warm Savannah's heart. It made her realize how fulfilling children could be. From seeing the girl's cheerful face in the morning to tucking her into bed at night made Savannah yearn for a sweet daughter like Lindsey...

She entertained the prospect of starting a different life. Having plenty of time promoted plenty of notions, crazy or not. Something Emily said hung in her mind, nettling her. "You can't always be a policewoman but you can always be a mom." Lindsey's company made Savannah consider chucking it to the department and begging Ennis to knock her up. She scheduled two weeks off from work so she'd use the time wisely to balance her decision.

Other issues demanding her attention revolved around weight. She chanced a trip to the scale which turned into a nightmare. After all the food Georgia brought and the nutritional "milkshakes" *and* lack of sufficient exercise, she'd gained three pounds already.

Not one of the pounds mattered when Dr. Wyatt called. Unfortunately Savannah was alone at the time. Ennis ran to Kroger's, probably for more nutritional supplements *and more food*, she assumed.

"The results are back," Wyatt said.

Her gut swirled up a storm of nausea in those brief seconds. The long-awaited moment arrived and she had to bear it alone. She'd waited impatiently for days to hear the results, now she was okay without knowing – at least a little longer until Ennis returned.

"I'm not ready for this." She stammered, "Ennis isn't here. We wanted to find out together."

"That's understandable. If you'd rather wait –"

"No, go ahead," she heard herself say. "I need to know." She couldn't judge Wyatt's tone. On the job she could detect certain inflections when people spoke. Their voices gave them away if they lied or tried to bend the truth. Dr. Wyatt was an enigma. He must be one hell of a poker player, she thought. The one aspect she learned was the pause. When he paused, look out. This time he did not pause, "The results came back negative. The lymph biopsy is cancer free and now we concentrate on radiation treatments. Now you've finally got good news to share."

The nausea continued plaguing her. It was too easy. It was too quick. It was all wrong, she feared. "Are you sure it's negative? There's no mistake? They made that mistake with my mother."

"Savannah, relax. I'm sure. I sent it to two pathologists to be certain. After your follow-up appointment we'll discuss a date to begin treatments."

The instant she hung up the phone, she began crying. The uncontrollable tears flowed like a veritable river and she thanked God for yet another miracle.

18

Lindsey spent another night with her aunt and uncle. It suited Savannah just fine since her niece seemed to feel at home with them. The few nights she stayed had been the longest she and Savannah spent together at one time. Savannah hated to see Lindsey leave for any reason, whether a simple trip to the store or worse, to go home.

Despite Leah's worries, the girl's behavior was exemplary and much more adult than either parent gave her credit. So much that Ennis felt comfortable going to work around noon while Lindsey stayed with her aunt. The ten day checkup lingered less than a week away but her niece treated her like she'd been home from the hospital less than a day.

Lindsey approached the fish bowl containing two bubble eye goldfish – fish she'd gifted to her aunt and uncle months before. The fish swam toward her begging for food. She obliged them by sprinkling the flake food across the top of the water, "My new fish are happy. Santa put ten in the tank you got me. Daddy's afraid they'll all have babies."

Lounging on the couch as per her young nurse's instructions, Savannah chuckled, "That sounds like Seth."

Lindsey watched the fish waggle their way to the top to eat, "Are you gonna have a baby, Aunt Vanna?"

Savannah fought the urge to swallow her tongue. Of all things, why did Lindsey ask that? "No, honey, someday Uncle Ennis and I will have babies, just not right now."

"Aunt Georgia said the doll she gave me would help me take care of your baby when you have one. My doll wets and cries, you know."

"Yes, you showed me your doll at Christmas." Georgia, being the extravagant type, never settled for a regular baby doll. No, she had to find the only doll that peed and cried. Not only that but the infant's skin felt too real, the chubby pink cheeks and tiny nose looked eerily genuine. An unsuspecting Savannah made over the pretty doll on Christmas Day and held it like a real infant sleeping peacefully in her arms. The joke was on her when the baby wet on her blouse then its eyes popped wide and the raucous crying began. If looks could've killed, Georgia would have been seriously maimed.

"Will you let me babysit when you have your baby? I'll take good care of it."

Why the sudden interest in babies, Savannah ventured no guess. Her niece zeroed in on the issue and until they exhausted her curiosity, Lindsey would keep mentioning it. "Of course, silly. You're my number one choice."

"Are you gonna quit your job and have babies soon?"

Georgia. That's who started this interrogation. Savannah's anger temporarily rose at her older sister's nosiness and the fact she enlisted their niece in her campaign. "I don't know yet, sweetheart. I'm still thinking on it. Say," she tried to change the subject, "are the fish doing okay? You're our resident expert on that too."

She seemed pleased, "They're big and happy." Lindsey kept watching the fish swim, "I'm gonna be Martha Washington in the school play."

"I heard you got the female lead. I can't wait to see you."

"It's gonna be in Feb-rary," Lindsey struggled with the month's name again then just shrugged and settled for, "President's Day. Daddy said you wouldn't come 'cause you'd feel bad."

Seth's assumption initially upset her. She was tired of people telling her what to do and when to do it – or whether she should do it at all. Her well meaning brother, in his inelegant manner, tried to excuse her from attending. What he overlooked in his haste was the fact she needed diversion, not rest. Lindsey worked hard to land the role of Martha Washington. Out of twenty-six other girls, she'd won the part. Savannah remembered how excited Lindsey was. She'd called her aunt after school and raved about it for an hour so no, Savannah wouldn't miss the play for the world. She assured Lindsey, "I'd never miss your play, sweetie. Tell your daddy I'll be there."

The guarantee perked the girl up. She smiled back at her, "I told him you'd come but he never believes me 'bout nothin'." She glanced at the clock, "Aunt Vanna, is it two-ish yet?"

For some reason, her usual title now shortened to a version of what Savannah's cousin Bobby addressed her as. Ever since she could remember, Bobby called her "Vanna" and now Lindsey's "Aunt Savannah" abbreviated to "Aunt Vanna" since the surgery. Evidently Lindsey found the nickname appealing for some reason.

The "two-ish" phrase caught her as odd though. Lindsey continued, "Uncle Ennis said to give you the milkshake and vitamin around two-ish. Is it two-ish yet?"

A quick glance at the clock revealed the time as one forty-two, "Close enough. 'Two-ish' is Texan for 'around two o'clock'."

When Lindsey glanced back, confusion ruled her sweet little face. Savannah realized the child took her seriously so she corrected herself, "It's not really Texan but that's what he means."

Her niece replaced the lid on the fish food, sat it down and skipped to the kitchen, "I like being a nurse."

"I couldn't ask for a better one." Or a more thorough one. The girl stuck religiously to Leah's instructions and when Savannah bellyached about something, Lindsey used "Mama said" as a backup. Seth turned out to be right. The word "no" was unacceptable in any language at any time.

Lindsey emerged holding the "milkshake" in one hand, a multi-vitamin in the other. Savannah thanked her, took the glass.

With her strictest pose, Lindsey policed her until she swallowed the vitamin. Savannah offered, "Wanna check and make sure I took it?"

The girl shook her head, "I trust you."

She sat the glass on the end table, "Glad someone does."

Lindsey piled up beside her on the couch, snuggled against her aunt. Savannah put her arm around her, drew her closer.

"I'm glad you're okay," the girl said, her voice a near whisper.

"Me too, sweetheart." She took a sip from the glass then finished, "Now I can see you go to college, get married and have a dozen kids that are as pretty as you.”

“Eww…” Lindsey wrinkled her nose, “I’m not gettin’ married. Boys are gross.”

A slow, secret smile crossed Savannah’s lips. In her youth, she said approximately the same thing. “They don’t stay gross. Look at your daddy and Uncle Ennis. They were boys once.”

Using her finger as a pen, the girl began drawing patterns on Savannah’s thigh, “They’re different.”

Taking another sip, Savannah observed the small fingertip methodically write an “L” then an “I” and the rest of Lindsey’s name. She sensed her niece gathering the courage to broach a particular subject. Savannah prayed it wasn’t about retiring or having babies. All in good time, she’d tell the girl. All in good time….

The finger now snaked back and forth into an “S” then an “A” and “V”. Halfway through Savannah’s name, Lindsey asked, “Do you believe in angels?”

The question temporarily took her aback. An eerie flash of déjà vu materialized of another little girl about Lindsey’s age asking that very same question. But, unlike then, this time Savannah’s answer came quick and exact, “Actually, I do. Why?”

“I saw one.”

“Where did you see the angel?”

“I saw it at the hospital.” Then as if defending her statement, she said, “Dylan saw it too. He called it a bird.”

Savannah figured the girl saw an angel statue in the hospital entry or the chapel. Angel images weren’t exactly scarce in those places. Before answering, she analyzed the phrasing of the question. Lindsey specifically asked "Do you believe in angels", not "have you seen angels". Savannah eased into the details, "Was it in the chapel?"

Lindsey shook her head, "Nuh-uh. She was floatin' above your bed. She came in with you, after your operation. She was pretty and had big ol' wings."

Savannah remembered seeing her mother standing behind R.J. and Georgia. Not some translucent image of her. Charlene was a real flesh and blood presence, just as if the clock rolled back in time. Had Lindsey and Dylan seen her too? And how – if it was even possible?

"You don't believe me," Lindsey pouted and crossed her arms. "That's why I didn't tell Daddy or Mama. They'd laugh."

Taking stock of her niece's expression – a youthful disappointment and defeat culminating in a puffed out lower lip and lowered head verged on comical – if the subject hadn't been so serious. With her arm still around the girl's shoulders, Savannah patted her, "Honey, I'm certainly not laughing. In fact, I do believe you."

Lindsey's brown eyes rounded, her mouth dropped open, "You do?" When her aunt nodded with no hint of humor, she proceeded with renewed enthusiasm, "She wasn't flappin' her wings though. She was just floatin' there." Silence ensued then, "You know what's weird?" She waited another appropriate amount of time for the mysteriousness to engage her aunt, "She looked like Aunt Georgia."

The gravity of Lindsey's description gripped Savannah as hard as seeing the image of Charlene in her hospital room. Her mother *had* visited her. No amount of others explaining it away or denying it, Charlene was with her, watching over her.

"Aunt Vanna, it couldn't have been Aunt Georgia so who was it?"

A thoughtful smile curved Savannah's mouth, "My guardian angel."

J.L. Lemon lives in Texas surrounded by a loving and supportive family, two adorable and devoted puppies, and hordes of garden gnomes.

Before 2002, J.L. Lemon wrote opinions and product reviews for an online consumer guide. When fellow reviewers cited the author's knack for humor, she decided to return to writing fiction. Along with the standalone title Second Chances, she's published 6 books in the Savannah Stories Series with 3 more in the works. For more titles from J.L. Lemon, please visit:

www.geocities.com/authorjllemon
www.geocities.com/upatmidnightpublishing

www.ingramcontent.com/pod-product-compliance
Lightning Source LLC
Chambersburg PA
CBHW050509260626
47157CB00004B/1256

9 780979 611766